THE SWEET TALKER

BOSTON HAWKS HOCKEY

GINA AZZI

The Sweet Talker

Copyright © 2021 by Gina Azzi

All rights reserved.

This is a work of fiction. Names, characters, businesses, places, events, locales, and incidents are either the products of the author's imagination or used in a fictitious manner. Any resemblance to actual persons, living or dead, or actual events is purely coincidental.

1

INDY

"You're coming out tonight," my cousin Claire demands, glancing at me in the reflection of her bedroom mirror. A mascara wand hovers in her hand and her tongue peeks out between her lips as she applies a second coat.

I flop back against her bed, staring at the glow stars that decorate her ceiling. We placed them there one summer, over a decade ago, and she's never taken them down. "I can't. I have work to catch up on."

"Too bad. You're too young and too hot to never get laid."

I snort, dropping my hand over my face. "I get laid." My voice is defensive, and as soon as Claire starts laughing, I join in.

I turn my head to meet her eyes in the reflection of the mirror. We're both sporting goofy grins. She jabs her mascara wand at me in the reflection. "Yeah? When was the last time you did it?"

I groan, yanking my gaze back to the ceiling. At least the glow stars aren't judgey. I don't answer Claire's question aloud but mentally, I tally up the months. There have been seven of them. Seven months since I had sex. It wasn't even good sex. More comfortable, one last hurrah before I relocate to Boston, see-ya-when-I-see-ya sex with Chris, the guy who conveniently lived down the street and was usually around for a casual hook-up. My closest childhood friend, Aiden, choked on his beer when I told him about my fling with Chris. He still hasn't stopped teasing me about it.

I wrinkle my nose. Meh, thinking of Chris as my last sexual partner is depressing on several levels.

Six months ago, when I landed in Boston for a new job, as an assistant professor at Brighton University, I swore to myself I'd turn over a new leaf. Now that I am on the tenure-track, I reasoned, I can stop being a self-isolated workaholic. My plan was to embrace the city, meet new people, and not keep myself locked in the library, researching, writing, and publishing. My plan failed.

The bed dips beside me. Claire's deep blue eyes peer into mine, determined, with just a hint of compassion. "I know you're working your ass off because you're intimidated."

"I'm the youngest assistant professor Brighton's ever hired."

"But you're qualified and competent. You're prepared for this job, Indy."

I shrug, not voicing how unprepared I feel. I've worked hard to secure this position but now that I have it, I feel a pressure to work even harder to prove that I can keep it. To show the administration that I was the right choice, that even though I'm only twenty-seven, I'm committed to academia.

Claire rolls her eyes. "You may be a prim and proper professor now but—"

"I'm not *that* prim and proper."

Her lips quiver with laughter. "Indiana, you are my favorite girl cousin."

"I'm your only girl cousin."

Claire ignores me. "I can't let you wallow away into nothing. Besides, I *need* a wing woman. Ever since Savannah abandoned me by gallivanting off to New York—"

"Mike got traded." I point out that my cousin Savannah, Claire's older sister, didn't move by choice. Her husband was traded by the Boston Hawks to the New York Sharks halfway through last hockey season.

Claire dismisses my logic and ticks on her fingers. "And Rielle is too busy working to have a life—"

"She's up for a promotion," I cut in, sticking up for Claire's best friend who has been working around the clock lately. Impressively, even more than me.

Claire glares at me. "My point is, *everyone* is ditching me and you have the shittiest excuse. The academic year started like, five seconds ago—"

"Three weeks."

"You're coming out tonight and we're celebrating," she concludes, hopping from the bed and striding to her closet. Claire pulls out a short, tight, black dress I would never wear and waves it around. "Put this on."

I laugh, pulling myself into a seated position, and play along. "What exactly are we celebrating?"

"Your new life. I love you, Indiana, but real talk, workaholic, stressed-out, type-A you is not a good look. You have a real job, which is more than I can say, and you're in a new city. You need to put yourself out there and mingle a little. Maybe you'll even meet someone." She eyes me hopefully, making the dress dance on the hanger.

I offer my cousin a half smile and weigh her words. She got me with the "real job" bit, which I'm sure she did on purpose, knowing my compassionate side would kick in. Since her college graduation in May, Claire's been freelancing but the work hasn't been steady. In fact, it's been so

unreliable that she moved back home with my aunt and uncle,
which pains her on a cellular level.

She widens her baby blues at me and I groan, dragging
myself to stand. But inside, a thrill shoots down my spine. It's
been ages since I've had a proper girls' night with Claire. My
cousin is fun, outgoing, and the life of the party. She's also
right. I do need to put myself out there and make some new
friends, meet some new people, and socialize like a normal
twenty-something.

For the past eight years, school was my entire life. Every
semester, I stacked my course load. I spent my summers
completing summer sessions on campus and my winter and
spring breaks contributing to research projects abroad. Gradu-
ating with my PhD in political science in January was my
greatest accomplishment until I secured an assistant professor
position at Brighton and moved to Boston in April. Since then,
I've been preparing for this next chapter and now, it's here. As
Claire kindly pointed out, I'm boring and predictable. My social
life revolves around my family members and a trusty planner.

If it weren't for weekly dinners with my family and
Claire's obligatory weekly retail therapy, I probably wouldn't
have gone out at all over the summer. A smile spreads across
my face. I deserve a night out, don't I? Besides, next week,
I'll be back in the classroom and focused on a research trip
I'm planning for a handful of students over winter break. I
can take this weekend to have a little fun. After all, didn't I
tell my freshman *Intro to Political Theory* the same thing?
"Okay."

Surprise flares in Claire's eyes. She thrusts the hanger
toward me, and when I take it, she lets out a loud whoop.
Laughing, I drop the dress on the bed and duck into the bathroom. I study my limp, brown hair, dull green eyes, and plain

face. While I'm not unfortunate-looking, I haven't put much effort into my appearance for a long time and it shows. Jesus, are my eyebrows touching? Cringe. Flipping on the faucet, I scrub my face clean and help myself to Claire's products, tweezers included. Then, I waltz into Claire's room and plop down.

"Make me over," I demand.

Her eyes widen and dazzle, deep blue like sapphires. "Indy, are you sure?"

I nod.

She squeals, "Oh my God. Tonight is going to be the best!"

DAD AND UNCLE JOE frown when Claire and I bound down the stairs, but Mom and Aunt Mary smile. The kitchen is already spotless from our weekly family dinner and our parents hold a drink in hand, talking and relaxing the way they have since Mom and Dad followed me to Boston over the summer.

"You look beautiful, Indy," Mom compliments as Dad scowls at my dress.

Aunt Mary's grin softens. "Absolutely gorgeous, girls. Where are you headed?"

"The Hawks are having a team kick-off at Firefly," Claire answers, filling up a glass of water and taking a long sip. "Austin said we could come."

"Oh, good." Dad breathes a sigh of relief that Austin, Claire's brother and the captain of the NHL team the Boston Hawks, will be present at the club tonight.

"Austin will keep an eye on them," Uncle Joe says,

although I think he's trying to convince himself more than Dad.

I roll my eyes, stashing my driver's license and a debit card into the small purse Claire lent me. "You realize we're adults, right? I'm going to be twenty-eight in a few months."

"And I'm moving out as soon as I can afford it," Claire announces.

Dad chuckles. "But you'll always be my little girl, Indy."

Claire snickers.

"Besides, I know hockey players." His tone turns hard, no doubt remembering all the wild escapades of his long career in the NHL. Dad, a hall of fame inductee and lead scorer for the Tampa Reds, can recount a staggering number of failed marriages and relationships gone wrong from his years in the league. His and Mom's enduring thirty-plus-year marriage is somewhat of an anomaly.

"No worries there," I scoff.

Aunt Mary stands, brushing her fingers through my hair. "Have fun tonight, Indy. You've been working so hard. You deserve a night out."

Mom lifts her wine glass in agreement. "Be safe, girls. If you need a ride—"

"Our Lyft is here," Claire interrupts, clutching my forearm and leading me toward the door. "If we need anything, we'll call," she reassures our parents, who still treat us like kids, probably because Claire is a wild card and I'm an only child. "I'm sleeping at Indy's tonight," she hollers over her shoulder as we slip outside.

Once we're settled in the Lyft and heading toward downtown Boston, Claire grins at me. "Wait 'til you see some of the Hawks' players." She fans herself.

I roll my eyes. "You know I'm not into hockey players. Not anymore." My first love, first heartbreak, first everything is now a defenseman on the Vancouver Eagles. After our very painful and public breakup two years ago, I swore off hockey players for good. Since then, I haven't been tempted once and I doubt tonight will be any different. If there's anything I've learned from being Dad's daughter and then dating Jace, it's that the stable and reliable lifestyle I crave doesn't mix with the NHL.

"Jace was a dick. Not all hockey players are like him."

I ignore her statement. "You can have your pick, Claire."

Her eyes dim and she turns to look out the window.

Uh-oh. For years, Claire has secretly pined over Austin's best friend and Hawks left winger Easton Scotch. Easton and his brother Noah have been fixtures at my aunt and uncle's home since bunking with Austin at hockey camp when we were all teenagers. Every summer, during our family trip to Boston, the Scotch brothers were present. Crushing on your brother's best friend is never easy, but with Easton's trip to rehab last year, Claire's complicated feelings became even messier.

I elbow her in the ribs until she turns toward me. "How's he doing?"

She sighs, knowing I'm asking about Easton. Other than me, Rielle, and Savannah, no one knows that Claire has been hung up on East for all these years. "Fuck if I know. He's barely spoken to me over the past year. Not since he came home from rehab."

"Have you seen him since the season ended?"

She shakes her head, her expression guarded.

Sensing she doesn't want to talk about Easton when we're about to embark on a night out, I ask, "Are you sure Austin doesn't mind that we're coming tonight?"

Claire laughs. "Oh, he's going to be pissed."

"What? You said—"

"Yeah, so our dads wouldn't worry. There's no way Austin wants us at Firefly tonight. Not when the team is getting together for the first time since the off-season. They're going to be partying hard and the puck bunnies are going to be swarming." She grins mischievously, shrugging one shoulder. "But once we're there, he's not going to turn us away."

I shake my head at my cousin, impressed. "You're evil."

"I'm resourceful. We're out for the night, we're going to have fun, and if we're lucky, we're going to *get* lucky."

Tossing my head back, I laugh. Claire doesn't join in.

"Wait, you're serious?"

She smirks in response.

2

NOAH

T he club is dark and loud, a perfect backdrop for poor decisions.

The section I'm in, a private, roped-off space our team captain Austin arranged, is exclusive in a way that permits regrets while keeping them private. I tip back my gin and tonic, letting the alcohol burn through my veins. At the very worst, I'll wake up with a hangover. Meanwhile, if my brother were here tonight instead of detoxing in rehab, a g and t would be the first domino in a destructive maze straight to rock bottom. Irony.

I drain the glass, rattling the ice as I set it down on a side table and gesture to a cocktail waitress milling about that I'll take another.

Below the railing, puck bunnies clamor for attention, desperate for an invitation up to where the team is enjoying bottle service. Sweeping my gaze over the crowd, pulsing with the beat the DJ dropped, I search for tonight's pick.

For three years, I was a saint. Sure, I'd notice if a girl was smoking hot the same way I'd notice if a guy was jacked. But I wasn't interested in any of the women, and definitely not puck bunnies, because I had my perfect girl waiting at home. Six months ago, right after we lost the game to qualify for the play-offs, Courtney's perfection cracked when I discovered her serious reservations about marrying me. Courtney called off our wedding two weeks before the big day, leaving me publicly humiliated and personally devastated.

No matter how many women I've slept with over the past six months, and I'm ashamed to admit that I've lost count, none of them have held my interest beyond a sloppy hook-up. Still, I keep searching, as if a random screw will somehow heal a bit of my broken. It's bullshit, because Courtney has already moved on with a lawyer, the kind of guy that can provide the "steady" lifestyle she desires, and I've regressed, bouncing back to my mid-twenties, when I partied hard and fucked any willing bunny.

My teammates tell me I've dodged a bullet and while I believe them, it doesn't make the hurt easier to manage or the betrayal easier to swallow. The off-season was rough, a series of lonely nights and dark thoughts. Between Courtney's cold feet and Easton's hitting rock bottom, I've never been so elated for training camps to kick off. For the past three months, I've thrown myself into preparing for this season and with only two weeks to go until our season opener, I'm feeling optimistic for the first time in months.

"You good?" Austin asks, bumping me with his shoulder.

"Yeah, man. You?" I accept my refill from the cocktail waitress with thanks and take a large gulp.

"How is he?" Austin asks, lowering his voice. As my brother's best friend, Austin's concern is deeper than just hockey and what Easton's rehab means for this season. He's genuinely worried about East's recovery, same as me.

I glance around but no one is paying us any attention. Some of the guys on the team suspect that Easton isn't really sick tonight. Or that he is but it's not a flu-like virus. Coach Phillips is going to break the news next week once East makes it through detox. "He's managing," I say, keeping my response vague.

The truth is, I have no clue how East is fairing in rehab. I know that he's surviving but I haven't been allowed contact with him. Even when I'm given permission to see him, I don't know if he'll want to see me. Or, more accurately, if he'll want me to see him in rehab. After his stint in rehab last year, my brother could barely meet my eyes. Embarrassed and disheartened, he confided that his inheriting our father's alcoholic gene bothers him a hell of a lot more than I realized. He fears turning into our old man, a father with a sharp tongue and even sharper hands.

Next to me, Austin raises his glass to his mouth but before he drinks, he leans over the railing, muttering swear words.

I try to follow his line of sight to see what's got him heated but other than some hot girls, I come up blank. "What's wrong?"

"I'm gonna fucking kill my sister," he growls, waving over to the bouncer to let the girls up.

I laugh. Having spent many weekends at the Merricks', I know firsthand that before Savannah married Mike, she was outgoing but always listened to her brother's warnings. Claire, on the other hand, throws caution to the wind and pushes every one of Austin's buttons just to see how much she can get away with. In the next blink, Claire steps onto the landing and I feel Austin's pain.

Claire has always been beautiful but dressed the way she is tonight, every guy in here will be salivating over her.

"She does it on purpose, you know?" I tell my friend as he begins to stalk toward his sister. Claire purposely flirts with my brother all the time just to piss Austin off. I open my mouth to remind Austin of this but my words stall in my throat as I get a look at Claire's friend.

Damn. The woman is a knockout. Long, brown hair that falls like a curtain of curls around her shoulders, sparkling green eyes that dazzle even from across the room, and a body that makes my mouth water, with hips I'd like to sink my fingers into and a graceful neck I want to run my mouth over.

I grab Austin's forearm before he disappears. "Who's she with?"

"My cousin." He sounds genuinely angry but there's a hint of surprise in his tone too, like he wasn't expecting to see his cousin tonight.

I sure as hell wasn't prepared to see her either. "That's Indy?" I ask, recalling an entirely different version of the Indiana Merrick I remember from my teenage years. She would visit Boston with her parents every summer and sometimes our paths would cross but she always held herself back, as if she preferred to be on the periphery while Claire beamed as the center of attention. Indy always had her nose in a book, rarely drank with us, and constantly talked about a hockey player she was dating.

I swivel my neck around the room, waiting to see which one of the guys steps up to claim her but nobody makes a move.

No one except Austin who is now striding toward his female family members with barely concealed fury in his expression.

Amused, I follow behind him.

"What the hell are you doing here?" he hisses at his sister and cousin.

Claire rolls her eyes. "We came to troll."

Indy winces and I snicker, drawing her attention to me.

When her eyes meet mine, I feel like I've been sucker punched. Now that I'm closer, the vibrance of her green eyes is even more alluring. Deep and glowing, her eyes are the kind a man would willingly drown in. The kind that make it easy to forget the past and live in the moment, consequences be damned.

I blink, severing the connection while mentally swearing at myself. Indiana Merrick is the last woman I should sleep with. Well, Savannah and Claire are but they're more like sisters to me anyway. Forget the fact that Indy is Austin's cousin, she's also the daughter of NHL legend Jeremiah Merrick, hockey god and my childhood idol. No hockey guy in his right mind would try casual with Indy and right now, tonight is all I'm good for.

Austin pulls Claire to the side of the room, leaving Indy and me to chat.

"Hi." She smiles shyly, placing out a hand. "I'm not sure if you remember me—"

"It's good to see you again, Little Indy," I cut her off, using the teenage nickname she hated. I shake her hand with a grin and tip my head toward the railing so we're not in the center of the room.

She follows beside me and as we post up next to the railing that overlooks the dance floor, I gesture toward the cocktail waitress. "What are you drinking?"

"Uh, I'll take a vodka soda with lemon please," Indy orders.

I study her, noting how she fiddles with the strap of her purse, glancing around for her cousins, unsure of herself. "How long are you visiting for?" I ask, hoping to put her at ease.

Her face swivels back to mine, surprise in her expression.

"Oh, I live in Boston now. I moved here about six months ago."

"Really?" Now I'm surprised, wondering why Austin never mentioned it. Then again, maybe he did. My life has been a roller coaster since last season ended. "Did you move for a job?"

Relief crosses her face as she nods. "Yes. And thanks for making that assumption. I hate that everyone always thinks I moved for a guy."

I chuckle, liking how transparent she is. Honest. "What do you do?"

"I'm a professor."

"Really?"

She tucks a strand of hair behind her ear. "Yeah. I just started this school year. I'm teaching political science courses at Brighton."

"Wow," I say, impressed. I remember Indy being smarter than the rest of us but I had no idea she wanted to teach. "You already did your PhD?"

She blushes, dropping her gaze and nodding, as if I embarrassed her. Honest and modest.

"That's awesome." And then, hoping to make her laugh, "Any of the students hit on you yet?"

I grin as her laughter colors the air. Her eyes come back up, disarming me.

"No." She shakes her head. "They're mostly eighteen and nineteen. They're still too nervous about doing their own laundry for the first time and remembering my name to try anything like that." She wrinkles her nose. "Don't get me started on work. I know it's lame to gush about but it's pretty much the center of my life at the moment."

"No man demanding all your time?" I couldn't care less if

I'm being forward. How the hell is a woman who looks like Indy and has her brains, spark, and drive, single?

She bites her bottom lip. "No one worth mentioning." Her voice is coy and my grin widens.

The cocktail waitress appears and I take Indy's drink off the tray and pass it to her. When she accepts the glass, our fingers brush and a flicker of heat shoots down my arm. Raising my glass in her direction, I smile. "To your new job. Congratulations, Professor."

She tips her head in my direction, her eyes flaring with amusement. Clinking her glass against mine, Indy lifts the cocktail to her lips.

I stifle a groan at the visual before me. Her mouth is luscious, her eyes gleaming, and everything about her screams unattainable. After months of easy, available women, Indy unknowingly entices me.

She's the first woman I've met since Courtney who stirs something in my chest. *Longing*. One to know her better, not just undress her tonight. The realization is heady and dangerous. Still, I can't stop the thrill that blazes through my body like fire, making my fingers want to reach out and glide over her smooth skin.

The Indiana Merrick I remember was prudent and oblivious.

This version is just as sweet but wildly tempting.

A recipe for trouble.

3

INDY

Noah Scotch.

The second my gaze collides with his, I forget how to breathe. I remember the sweet talker with his rugged jawline and deep, chocolate eyes from my teenage years. Back then, Noah seemed so far out of my reach, it's like we weren't even in the same galaxy. The first time I met him at my aunt and uncle's house, I blushed and fumbled through the entire dinner. Noah sat beside me and when he reached for the grated parmesan cheese, his elbow ran down the length of my arm, causing goosebumps to break out over my skin.

He was the first guy I ever had a real crush on. Of course, it was harmless and innocent. Later that year, I met Jace and everything in the world seemed to melt away as I fell in love with him. But standing here now, with Noah looking at me like he's genuinely interested in hearing about my career, those old, delicious memories resurface.

"Can I ask you something?" he asks after we've been chatting for a solid fifteen minutes. By this time, my cousins have reappeared and disappeared several times. Luckily,

Austin acquiesced to Claire's demands to stay, although he's been watching my devious cousin like a hawk as she makes her rounds, laughing and flirting with all the hockey players.

"Sure," I say cautiously.

He rubs a hand along his jawline and I catch the movement, wondering, for one tiny instant, what it would feel like for his fingers to swipe across my cheek, dip down the column of my neck.

He clears his throat and I startle, flicking my gaze back to his but realize he's pondering how to pose his question.

"Just ask it." I flash him a smile.

He chuckles, the sound nervous. Shuffling forward half a step, he dips his head and I breathe in his scent. It's fresh like pinecones and mountain air and it makes my mouth water. "How do you balance it all? The commitment to your career and your social life and dating…I just, I wonder because I thought I was balancing it all fine and now…" he trails off, shaking his head. Pink stains his cheeks and I catch his embarrassment, softening to him even more because of it.

I tip back to peer into his eyes, surprised by his question. Not that I knew what he was going to ask but it definitely wasn't that. We just jumped from polite, comfortable chitchat to something deeper. I recall the headlines and social media stories surrounding Noah this summer. His fiancée Courtney cheated on him with a lawyer or engineer or something. I shuffle even closer to him, as if pulled by an invisible thread. One dipped in hurt and vulnerability, one seeking understanding and comfort.

His honesty spurs my own, even if it pains me to admit it out loud. "I don't."

Noah's brow furrows, as if my answer is confusing.

I clear my throat. "I don't balance it at all. My entire life revolves around my work, my research, that's it. Claire dragged me out tonight by sheer will and her ability to guilt trip."

The corner of his mouth turns up even though his eyes remain serious, disbelief ringing their edges. "Me too. Until Courtney I mean…I just, I was all about the job."

I take a long pull of my drink. "It's easier that way."

"Safer," he agrees, rattling the ice in his glass.

We stare at each other for a long beat, some type of understanding passing between us. "I'm sorry about Courtney."

He shrugs, glancing out over the crowd. "I'm not."

I raise an eyebrow, surprised.

"Don't get me wrong, I'm gutted about the way it went down. But I'm not sorry. I would much rather have understood her expectations, have her realize the type of life and future she wants, before we exchanged vows and not after, with a handful of kids in tow."

The thought of Noah as a dad causes my chest to ache. My God. Claire was right; I need a life. Still, I admire his rational outlook and I tell him as much.

He snorts, polishing off his drink. "I can say this now, six months later. Right afterwards"—he pauses, a darkness flaring in his eyes—"well, let's just say that *impressed* is not a word you would use to describe me."

I open my mouth to say something comforting when Austin appears and throws an arm across my shoulders. He tugs me toward a group of men I know by name from *SportsCenter* but have never met in person. "You moved here just as the season ended and everyone went their separate ways. Let me introduce you to the team, Indy."

I raise an eyebrow and glance up at Austin.

"Purely so they'll know better than to hit on you," he clarifies, making his intention known.

Tossing back my head, I laugh. Noah chuckles but Austin's expression remains serious.

My cousin leads me toward the guys but I glance over my shoulder at Noah who remains at the railing. His hand wraps around the metal bar as his head swivels in my direction. His expression is amused, a small smile playing over his mouth. But his eyes burn with intensity as they latch onto mine. They track my movement with a severity I'm unprepared for and a thrill shoots down my spine. Noah's gaze holds me hostage. Intense, heady, and hungry, this Noah rattles me even more than the boy I first crushed on.

***

"EASTON'S BACK IN REHAB!" Claire hisses at me. We're partially hidden, around the side of the bar, while Austin's teammates socialize and mingle. "I mean, I'm pretty sure he is. Panda told me but said it wasn't a confirmed thing but then, why else wouldn't he be here?"

Mingle is putting it politely. Several of the guys have their hands roaming the curves of beautiful women, no shame in their game, as they touch freely. Women perch on their laps, their clothes tighter than skin, their makeup expertly applied.

I can't tear my eyes away. I've spent the last several years locked in libraries, surrounded by guys in cardigans and girls who sport baseball caps on bad hair days. Or greasy hair days. The women surrounding me look like they never have a bad anything. They are mesmerizing. The guys think so too and a strange sensation ripples through my chest.

No wonder things with Jace and me didn't work out. I couldn't look like one of these girls with an entire team committed to my appearance, a la Sandra Bullock in *Miss Congeniality*.

"Indy! Did you hear me?" Claire shakes my hand, her eyes glazed. She stumbles and I grab her arm to keep her from teetering in her heels.

I wince, recalling Austin's best friend and Claire's number one crush. Easton Scotch is in a category all his own. Wild and reckless, he's a force on the ice and a hurricane off of it. Bad boy personified, he was always getting into some kind of trouble. Now, I recognize his teenage pursuits for what they are—a man trying to escape his demons. But years ago, I found him irritatingly rash and careless. Still, my chest aches for him and for Noah, knowing how close they are as brothers, and for Claire who continues to worry about East even while flinging herself at other men. "I heard you. I'm sorry, Claire," I say, studying my cousin.

For every drink I've consumed, she's had three. Frowning, I realize she's quite drunk.

Tears prick the corners of her eyes as she shakes her head. "What do you think triggered him? How do you think he is?"

I push her back into the corner, glancing around to make sure Austin hasn't spotted us. If he knows Claire is wasted and nearly sobbing, he'll drag us from Firefly and Claire will be doubly embarrassed tomorrow. "I'm not sure, Claire. But the good news is he's working on it. Rehab isn't a bad thing. It's a step on the path to recovery."

She squeezes her eyes shut, her black mascara smearing on her brow bone and beneath her eyelids. Jesus. I swipe a bar napkin from the bar and try to fix her face while shushing her. "Claire, Austin is going to haul you out of here if you don't pull it together."

"Ohmygod." She drops her head to my shoulder, swaying. "Do you think Austin knows?"

"Knows what?" Austin asks, sauntering up to us, his expression murderous.

"Claire drank a little too much. We're just having a moment." I grin, trying to play off Claire's wasted state.

Austin grumbles under his breath, looking over his shoulder. In an instant, Noah appears. "I'm going to take the girls home."

Claire shakes her head, her fingers gripping the material of my dress. "No. We want to stay."

"You can barely stand," Austin snaps.

She glances up, her eyes bleary, her makeup smeared. "Let Indy stay. She never goes out. Her vagina is going to close up if she doesn't get some good di—"

"Stop talking," Austin demands.

Holy shit. I'm going to kill Claire. I drop my face, knowing it's flaming from my chest to the tips of my ears. I can't believe Claire's drunk ass just outed me like that. But I can't deny it. Seven months is…seven months.

My skin flushes all over again.

Over the din of the chatter and the distant pulsing of the beat on the dance floor, I hear Noah and Austin exchange words.

In the next instant, Claire's being pulled from my arms as Austin supports her weight. He glances at me. "You want to stay, Indy?"

Not after Claire's public declaration. Right now, I'd like the ground to open and plunge me to Earth's core until the next century. I open my mouth as Noah says, "I'll make sure you get home."

My mouth snaps shut. I look around the private section we're enclosed in, the gorgeous women, the wildly attractive, muscular men, the plushness of the club. I am way out of my depth here. Way, way out of my comfort zone. I should leave. I should go back to my apartment and my reading chair and pour a glass of wine and lose myself in

Yuval Noah Harari's *Sapiens: A Brief History of Humankind*.

Claire pinches me, reminding me that I'm turning over a new leaf. Starting now.

"Sure," I hear myself say, still shocked that I'm agreeing to *this*.

Austin cuts Noah a look. "Keep an eye on her."

"Of course, man," he agrees, offering me a smile. "I promise, you'll have fun, Indy."

"I'm sure she will," Claire mutters.

Austin shakes his head, pulling her toward the exit. He points at me. "Call me if you need anything."

"I'll be okay, Aus." I wave him off. Even though I haven't spent a ton of time growing up around Austin, he's always looked out for me like I was his third sister. The same way Aiden does. The realization warms me up, filling a bit of my only-child void.

Noah shuffles forward, his fingers pressing into the small of my back. He dips his head. "Want a drink?"

I nod.

He steers me closer to the front of the bar. "We can leave whenever you want."

"Oh, I don't have to stay if you have," I pause, glancing around the space, "*plans*."

Noah chuckles, following my line of sight. "I didn't mean it like that. It's just, Austin told me this isn't really your scene. So, whenever you're ready to call it a night, tell me."

I scoff, pulling back and looking at him. "What? You're going to tell me this isn't your scene either?"

Chagrin flushes across his features and he flags down a bartender. "Nope. Lately this is too much my scene."

I blush at the meaning underlying his words and order a vodka soda.

Noah rests his lower back against the bar beside me. He crosses his arms over his chest, his biceps bulging. How do men make casual look so enticing? I tap my fingertips on the top of the bar, wracking my brain for something smart to say as Noah studies me.

The bartender slides over my drink. "Thanks," I say, picking it up, relieved I have something to do with my hands.

"You're the most interesting woman in here, Indy," Noah says after a beat.

I rear back, surprised, wondering if he's joking with me. But when I meet his gaze, his eyes are as black as midnight, intense and potent.

I take a long pull of my vodka soda, needing the liquid courage to interact with him.

Especially since I'm happy I decided to stay.

4

NOAH

I ndiana Merrick could tempt a saint.

While nearly every woman in the club tonight and definitely the women up here partying with the team would do almost anything to impress one of the guys, Indy sets herself apart.

She's dressed sexy as hell, with long, shapely legs, delicious curves, and hair I want to fist my hand in. But it's her face that's gold. Her damn expressions, so genuine and honest, ripple across her features with an openness that most of the women I know learned to conceal years ago.

Her eyes burn with curiosity and excitement and a self-consciousness that's more endearing than it should be.

"How do you like Boston?" I ask, wincing at how lame I sound. The truth is, I don't have much practice with small talk. Most people I interact with want something from me, like an autograph or tickets to a game. Most women I engage with offer something up on a silver platter, like an opportunity to get naked and not talk.

The thought rattles me a little. It's been too many years since I've had to put any type of work in with a woman and because Indy isn't a regular woman I can just sleep with and never see again, I feel out of my depth having a normal conversation.

"I like it." She wrinkles her nose. "Not a huge fan of winter so I'm not sure what the next few months are going to be like. But I like being closer to my cousins and aunt and uncle."

"And your parents moved up here too?"

She nods, taking another sip of her drink. "I guess in that sense I'm lucky to be an only. With Dad retired, they could move anywhere and they're pretty set on being close to me."

I scratch my cheek, wondering what the hell that must be like. My parents struggle to tolerate East and me for the one or two visits a year we make upstate. They would never move anywhere just to be closer to us, even if it was all expenses paid. I've never been my parents' focus or priority, just an added burden on the periphery of their lives that child services demanded they pay attention to every now and then. As long as East and I cut them monthly checks, they don't care about what's happening in our lives. "Yeah, I remember how much your dad would try to drag you to all our hockey camps whenever you guys came up to Boston in the summer."

Indy rolls her eyes. "He may have been mildly disappointed I turned out to be a girl more interested in ballet and books than in perfecting a slap shot."

I chuckle, recalling Indy sitting on the bleachers, her eyes scanning line after line, devouring chapters like it nourished her soul, while her dad ran an impromptu session that any of the players attending would talk about for the next year straight. Jeremiah Merrick is a hockey legend and while I'm sure part of him is disappointed that his only child couldn't care less about hockey, I doubt he was ever disappointed he had a daughter instead of a son. "Nah, your dad straight up dotes on you."

She blushes, grinning. "I am a massive daddy's girl."

"You and Claire and Savannah. I feel bad for the Merrick dads." I rattle the ice in my glass before draining my drink.

"Yeah. Our dads are pretty great. They give good advice."

"Such as?"

She wrinkles her nose. "Never date a hockey player."

I tip my head back and laugh, nodding in agreement with that nugget of wisdom. "Yeah, on that front, I'd bet your dad was relieved you were too lost in your books to pay attention to us on the ice, doing our best to impress you."

She quirks an eyebrow. "You guys tried to impress me?"

"All the time!" I turn toward her, so I'm facing her straight on. Even in her heels, the top of her head barely comes up to my chin. She's so petite, I could probably wrap my hands around her waist and my fingers would touch. It's strange, but the observation makes me feel even more protective of Indy than I did when Austin left her in my care. "Don't you remember those skating races we would have?"

She shakes her head, looking genuinely confused.

"Oh my God," I moan. "I don't know whether to be jealous that your fantasy fiction books were more interesting or impressed that you were that devoted to your reading and studies."

She blushes again, biting the corner of her mouth. It's sweet and tempting, contradicting gestures that make me want to wrap my arms around her for being so damn irresistible.

"Wait a minute." I frown, remembering the only guy I've ever heard her speak about. "Didn't you date a hockey player?"

Her blush deepens and a ripple of pain crosses her face,

her lips pinching. While I mentally swear at myself for bringing up some douche who obviously hurt her, I'd be lying if I didn't admit that my curiosity is piqued. What hockey player had a shot with Indiana and fucked it up for the rest of us?

"It didn't work out," she says softly, her fingers toying with the straw in her glass. She glances up at me, her eyes tender. "We were together for years and then he got drafted…" she trails off, shrugging. Even though I haven't seen her in years, even though I don't know her that well, it doesn't take a rocket scientist to realize he hurt her. And that whatever led to the demise of their relationship is a hell of a lot deeper than just him getting drafted.

I shuffle forward half a step, so close now that I can feel the heat of her body. My fingers run up the length of her arm and she tips her head back, meeting my gaze head-on. We're both a little tipsy now but I won't use that as an excuse. The truth is, my fingers itch to brush across her skin. I want to provide her even the smallest semblance of comfort, anything to make that look of dejection slide off her face.

"Who is he?" I growl, wondering if it's a guy I know. Is it someone I consider a friend? Or a player I can't fucking stand? The fact that I don't know irritates me.

She shakes her head. "It was a long time ago. We were kids."

I definitely know him. I wrack my brain, trying to guess, but come up blank. "What's his name?"

She rolls her lips together, pinning them between her teeth. Her green eyes are bright, shimmering with flecks of gold. "Jace Edwards."

I blanch, recalling the douchebag with perfect clarity. "From the Vancouver Eagles?"

She nods, her fingers twisting together in front of her waist, her empty drink placed back on the bar.

"He doesn't fucking deserve you," I bite out, not caring that I probably sound deranged. But Jace fucking Edwards? That dude cheats on every single woman I've ever seen him with. He's a shit boyfriend and an even shittier player. He didn't even start last season.

She winces. "You don't even know what happened."

I snort. I could guess what happened. He dipped his dick in another girl, or several girls, and one of them made sure Indy found out about it. Stupid guy is still playing the same dumb games with women, looking for some type of notoriety among his peers since he sure as hell can't get it on the ice. "You want to tell me?"

She shakes her head, her lips pressing together in a thin line.

My hand curves around her elbow. "I know Jace."

"I figured."

"I don't like him."

"Sorted that one out too."

"Your dad was right, Indy. Don't date hockey players."

She lifts her eyebrows, surprised. "Because you're all the same?"

"No." I shake my head. I haven't been a saint these past six months but I've never stepped out on any woman I was seeing exclusively. Not once. "We're not all the same. But you're too good for all of us. Maybe even for all the men on the planet."

She tips her head back and laughs, some of the sadness fading from her eyes. I can tell she thinks I'm messing with her but I'm dead serious. I don't know a guy worthy of Indiana Merrick with her sweet expressions and quirky habits. The women who would rather read *Harry Potter* at the

Stanley Cup Finals and study when her girl cousins were curling their hair for a night out. She's in a league all her own, one far, far removed from the NHL.

"Shots!" My teammate Torsten knocks into me from behind, pushing me into Indy's space.

My hands wrap around her waist to keep her from falling and I roll my back against the ledge of the bar, tucking her against my chest to keep her upright. She stumbles in her heels, a mixture of my knocking her off balance and the alcohol buzzing through both of our veins, causing us to falter. Once I find my footing, I hang onto Indy. I know I should drop my hands but she fits against my chest perfectly and it's nice, to hold on to a woman I genuinely like.

"You guys are in." Torsten snaps his fingers at us counting out how many shots to order.

"Oh no," Indy protests, taking a step forward. "I don't need one."

My hands slide to my sides as I watch her try to convince Torsten that she's not going to take a shot.

"You're Indiana Merrick, aren't you?" Torsten asks her, his gaze cutting from her to me and back again.

She nods, her brow furrowed as if wondering what that has to do with anything.

"Torsten Hansen." He holds out a hand.

"From Norway," Indy adds, shaking it.

Torsten grins. "So you've heard of me?"

"Saw that wicked slap shot against Chicago," Indy admits, causing Torsten's and my mouths to pop open.

"I thought you were too busy reading to watch hockey?" I place my hand in the small of her back, noting that Torsten catches the movement.

It's wrong, because I'm not laying claim to Indy.

And yet, I'm laying some type of claim to Indy because

no way in hell are any of my teammates touching her tonight. Or any night for that matter.

Torsten chuckles. "That was three seasons ago."

"I still remember the highlights." She waves a hand. "It's good to meet you. You should rush the puck more. You're really great at reading the ice and setting up the play. Don't pass up on opportunities to create offensive play. Lean into them." She gives him unsolicited advice and his mouth twists before a bark of laughter pours out.

He nods, agreeing with her observation. "Your dad tell you that?"

"Nah." She shakes her head, grinning at him cheekily. "That's all me."

"I'm impressed, Indiana," he says, flashing ten fingers to the bartender. "Patrón," he calls to the guy lining up shot glasses.

"It's just Indy," she says.

"What?" He turns back toward her.

"You can call me Indy," she repeats.

"Okay, Indy. Now that you've unmanned me by dissecting the weaker points of my game, you need to take a shot with me so I can somehow save face in front of this group."

She chuckles, shifting from one foot to the other before nodding in agreement.

"Line 'em up!" Torsten shouts, beckoning other guys from the team to step up to the bar.

When we're a group of ten, with little Indy Merrick in the center of us bickering and snickering players, we hold up our shot glasses.

Torsten glances at Indy expectantly. "What are we cheers-ing to?"

A wave of panic flares in her features but in a blink, she

pushes it down and replaces it with amusement. "To Torsten's slap shot!"

The guys all laugh with Torsten cracking up. A few of the guys drop interested glances Indy's way and I step even closer, making sure my body language signals that they need to back the hell up.

Indy, of course, is oblivious to all of this. Instead, she tosses back her shot and winces as the strong alcohol blazes down her throat.

Placing her shot glass back on the bar, she wipes the back of her hand across her mouth in a very unladylike gesture. I grin.

"That was awful," she says accusatorially.

"That was awesome," I say instead, enjoying tonight more than I have enjoyed any night in a long time.

Tequila shots. Vodka sodas. And it's a beer that puts me over the edge.

I am drunk. Not wasted like Claire, but tipsier than I've been since Savannah's bachelorette party three years ago. That night, I thought I was embarking on this exciting new path that was going to lead to an unbelievable, impactful job and a marriage proposal with my dream guy. Ha! I take another swig of beer.

Guys from Austin's team—Noah, Torsten, and the goalie everyone calls Panda—sit around me, chatting and laughing. While being around hockey players is nothing new, tonight feels different.

These guys have already made it. While they admire my dad, they're not talking me up for an autograph or a chance to meet him. All of them have met him dozens of times, worked hockey camps with him, and aren't starstruck anymore. They're also not tolerating me because I'm Austin's cousin, a new transplant to Boston.

They're genuinely interested in the words coming out of my mouth. The conversation is easygoing and effortless. I feel like one of the girls I always used to admire from afar, a girl like Claire or Vanny. One who could sit amidst a group of strong, successful, desirable men and be comfortable in their skin.

Buzzed on a mixture of alcohol and a heady sense of confidence, I'm having more fun than I have in years.

"You *dated* Jace Edwards?" Torsten asks next to me, his face contorting in disgust.

I giggle. Giggle! "He's not that bad."

"The fact that you have to say that means he's even worse," Torsten points out.

Tipping my head to the side, I nod, agreeing that his logic makes sense. Jace Edwards really does suck.

Him cheating on me devastated me. He broke my heart and dashed all the dreams I was conjuring up about our future. But that wasn't the worst part. The worst part is the way he chipped at my confidence for years, always nagging that his career was the one that mattered, that his goals were more important than mine. He made an impressive case for why his future was so much brighter than anything I would accomplish, and at some point, I started to believe him. I began to make myself smaller so that he could feel bigger. By the time he publicly cheated on me with a girl that should grace the cover of a magazine, my self-confidence was shattered. I spent the past two years trying to make myself even more invisible and sticking to the only thing I'm good at: school.

The reminder makes my stomach twist and the club to spin around me, colors and sounds blurring together. I grip the underside of the bar to keep from sliding off the barstool and feel the heat of Noah's body as he steps up behind me.

Torsten is chuckling at whatever Panda is saying so when

Noah's palm rests in the center of my back and he dips down, whispering, "You okay?" in my ear, no one notices.

Goosebumps travel over my skin as his breath skates over the shell of my ear. I turn my head until his lips nearly brush my cheek.

"Indy? You doing okay?" he repeats, his mouth so close to my skin that the wildly irrational thought of turning into his touch crosses my mind.

I nod, feeling Noah's hand slide up my back, under the curtain of my hair, until his fingers are cradling my head. He turns my face to his, his eyes like two pools of black. They flicker with worry and flare with heat. Such contradicting emotions and yet, both send a thrill throughout my body.

"Are you ready to head out?" he asks, his fingertips brushing along my scalp, his hand traveling from my head to the side of my face, cupping my cheek. My eyes flutter closed, and this time, I can't stop myself from leaning into his touch.

He swipes his thumb along my cheekbone and I force my eyes to open. "Okay," I say.

A soft smile plays over his lips. "Okay, babe. Let's say good night."

Babe. It drops from his lips so casually, he must say it to hundreds of women. Thousands. But the look in his eyes when he said it to me was anything but casual and I latch onto that instead.

We say good night with Torsten kissing my cheek and Panda giving me a big hug. They both give Noah extra-long glances but he ignores them, focused on guiding me out of the roped-off section, down the winding staircase, and out the back entrance of Firefly.

"You called a car?" I ask, surprised that a driver is already waiting for us.

Noah shrugs. "I always keep a driver on standby for nights like these. Something is bound to go sideways." He holds open the back door and ushers me inside.

I slide all the way across the bench even though I expect him to take the passenger seat. Surprise and excitement lick low in my stomach when Noah climbs in beside me and closes the door. With his too big frame folded up in the small space, our knees touch. I place my palm down in the space between our thighs, and as the driver pulls out of the parking lot, Noah's large hand covers mine.

"You have fun tonight?" he asks, his gaze curious.

"I really did." I'm grateful for the delicious buzz still swirling in my bloodstream because otherwise this—being alone and so close to Noah Scotch—would fill me with nerves instead of anticipation.

"Where to, Scotch?" the driver calls over his shoulder.

Noah looks at me. "What's your address, Indy?"

I rattle it off and the driver nods, turning up the song he's listening to. But a moment later he swears.

"There's an accident on Devonshire and Congress. Tremont and Blossom are at a standstill." He gazes at us in the rearview mirror. "Up to a fifty-minute delay. What do you want to do?"

I freeze, my limbs locking down as I process this news. Are we going to sit in traffic? Is Noah going to offer me to come to his place? The idea excites me and I sit perfectly still, waiting for Noah to say something.

"We can wait it out if you want, Indy. But I vote that you come back to my place and we crash." He glances at his watch. "It's already after two."

The thrill in my stomach flares up into my chest and down into my legs. I clear my throat. "That's fine."

Noah informs the driver of our decision. As he speaks, his

hand closes over mine, holding on to my fingers, his thumb drawing lazy circles over my knuckles. He doesn't let go until we pull up in front of a sweet brownstone in Beacon Hill.

"Wow." I glance at him. "You live here?"

"Me and East."

"I didn't know you lived with your brother," I say, sliding from the back seat and shivering from the breeze. While it's not yet winter, it's a hell of a lot colder than I'm used to. I moved to Boston in April from the heat and sun of Florida. My southern roots aren't well-adjusted to the cold yet.

Noah wraps an arm around me, as if the bulk of his muscles could block the wind. Hell, they probably could. He exchanges a few words with the driver and then guides me up to the front entrance.

"East and I bought this place together years ago. He was living here solo for the past two years when Courtney and I bought a home." He grimaces and I suddenly wish I didn't say anything about him living with Easton. "But I sold it after…"

I nod, not needing him to elaborate on that sentence. "It's beautiful."

He shoots me a grateful look. "Thank you." He punches in the code for the front door and pushes it open. I step inside and Noah enters quickly behind me, turning off and resetting the alarm.

He flips the lights on and my breath lodges in my throat. His home is more than beautiful. It's like stepping into the spread of a design magazine.

The bones of the house, old and charming and historic, have been well-preserved and blended with contemporary materials and functional amenities. Exposed brick blends with industrial-style lighting. A real wood fireplace is book-ended by built-in shelves with hockey awards and classic literature. An open floor plan is created from the history of over a hundred years of separated rooms, each with a specific function.

"This is amazing," I say, spinning around in a circle.

Noah blushes and it's the sweetest thing ever. "It was mostly East."

I push at his chest playfully. "Stop being so modest."

He chuckles, grabbing my hand and pulling me closer until I crash into his chest, my breasts pushing into his abdomen.

He glances down, his eyes sparking as they catch on my now pushed-up cleavage, before he drags his gaze up to mine. One of his hands settles on my waist. "I should get you some pajamas. And water." He doesn't make a move to do either and I don't say anything to encourage him to remove his hand.

Because right now, I want nothing more than to feel his hands on me. To feel his fingers caress my skin, to know what it tastes like to have his tongue coax in between my lips and dance with mine.

A small sigh escapes my mouth and Noah's jaw tightens, his gaze sharpening.

I reach up and my hand curls around his forearm, keeping his hand anchored to my hip.

We stare at each other, our elevated breathing mixing in the space between us.

"You don't date hockey players," he reminds me, his words a whisper but forcefully said, like he's trying to remind himself too.

I lick my bottom lip and his eyelids drop to half-mast.

"You don't really date at all," I reply, my voice huskier than I've ever heard it.

He closes his eyes, dropping his forehead to mine. "I

can't do this with you, Indy. Not tonight." He rolls his forehead gently and I shuffle even closer.

"Not tonight or not ever?" I ask, not caring how desperate
I sound. I'm grateful for the liquid courage pumping through
my blood. It's been too long, maybe even my entire life, since
I've felt desire like this. It's thick in my veins, swimming like
molasses. But my mind is made up, my head clear that Noah
Scotch could make me feel like I've never felt before.

I know with certainty that his kiss would put all of Chris's
to shame, that his touch would erase any memory of Jace, that
his body shadowing mine would be the greatest ecstasy I've
ever had.

Right now, tipsy and needy, I want it more than oxygen.

I tip my chin up a fraction, lining up our lips until they
nearly touch. Our breaths are like sweet caresses, our fingers
still digging into each other, holding on to the thread of
control that frays with each exhale.

"Fuck," Noah swears right before he frames my face with
his large hand and presses his lips to mine.

I kiss him back eagerly and I know I catch him off guard
by the way he automatically slants my head in his hand and
deepens our connection. He tastes like beer and peppermint;
he smells like pinecones and winter.

I moan as his tongue dances with mine and feel his hand
slide all the way around my waist, until I'm arching my body
into his. My arms wrap around his shoulders, my hands
clasping behind his neck.

He kisses me desperately, like he thinks he'll never kiss
me again.

Heat pools between my thighs and my nipples tingle,
desperate to be touched. In fact, I feel like I'm vibrating with
need, needy for Noah's skilled fingers to provide a relief I
haven't experienced in too damn long.

I whimper and he swears, ending our connection as quickly as it started and taking a step back. He stares at me, his eyes wild, his chest heaving, his hands clenched into fists.

I raise my hand to my mouth, coming back to the moment, coming back to the reality where I desperately threw myself into the arms of hockey heartthrob, Noah Scotch.

Embarrassment washes through me and my gaze flickers to the front door behind Noah. For fuck's sake, we didn't even make it past the foyer. I make a move to start for the door but Noah growls, causing me to freeze.

"You're staying here tonight," he says the words decisively, no hesitation in his expression. "But we can't go there, babe." He gestures between us, shaking his head.

I bite the corner of my lip, my arms crossing in front of my chest, practically hugging myself. Shit, I messed up. I took advantage of Noah's kindness. From his looks all night, I know he finds me attractive but that doesn't mean he wants to sleep with me. I'm nothing like the women he's usually pictured with, about as far from his ex-fiancée as one could be.

Noah's gaze softens as he studies me. He strides forward, eating up the space between us and wraps his arms around me, holding me. "You'll never understand how badly I want you right now. But you deserve more, Indiana. Much more than me, and a hell of a lot more than what I'm capable of giving. All I've got is tonight."

I glance up at him, noting the way his Adam's apple bobs. His voice is sincere and I can tell he means, truly believes, the words he's saying.

The thing is, his words don't bother me. They're not the issue. Jace taught me better than to hitch my star to a hockey player. My star can blaze all on its own. But right now, I *want* Noah.

I want the wild, uninhibited, carefree, live-in-the-moment fun I've denied myself for far too long. I have a history with Noah, enough to know he's a good man and one hell of a good time.

So I open my mouth and say, "What if tonight is all I want?"

He swears, his eyes blazing with heat I feel in my veins.

Grabbing the front of his shirt, I pull him closer and kiss him hard, until his lips mold to mine and he carries me up the stairs, to his bedroom.

He tosses me in the center of his bed and I'm shimmying out of my dress as fast as he's pulling his sweater over his head. He loses his pants next and I giggle. I giggle! Because this moment is fun and exciting and overflowing with sexy expectations and nothing else.

This is what I've been missing? I could slap myself for passing up on nights like these all throughout college.

Noah pounces on me, his expression playful. "You sure about this, Little Indy?"

I lie down and hook my heels around his back, pulling him closer. Between the liquid courage of tequila, the heady look in Noah's eyes, and the sweet promise of living in the moment, I nod. "So ready, Scotch. Give me your best."

He chuckles even as his eyes burn. "Promise, baby."

Then he dips his head, kisses me hard, and lights me up like a firework finale on the Fourth of July.

6

NOAH

My mouth feels like cotton and a dull throb aches behind my eyes when I wake up the following morning.

Shit. How much did I drink last night?

Slowly, memories of the evening thread together in my mind. Austin organizing a team night out. Firefly, dark lights and a pulsing beat. Shots with Torsten. And Indy.

Indy! I sit straight up in my bed and swing my legs to the side of the mattress.

Last night, I kissed Indiana Merrick and it was spectacular. Then, I fucked her seven ways 'til Sunday in my goddamn bedroom.

I turn around, noting the empty side of the bed with an indent still on the pillow. Shit. Where'd she go?

For a guy who has been with too many women to count, none of them, not even Courtney, made quite an impression on me in such little time.

I pull on some sweats before I head downstairs and into the kitchen.

"Indy?" I call out but the house is silent. Did she ghost me?

I chuckle, shaking my head. Little Indy has definitely grown up. In fact, if any other girl ghosted me after a night out followed by hot sex, I'd be relieved. But with Indy, I'm both disappointed and impressed.

My fascination with her heightens when I notice that the Nespresso machine is open and a rinsed-out mug sits next to the sink. She didn't even try to sneak out but had a leisurely morning on her way out the door. I shake my head and chuckle. Swiping a mug from the cabinet, I pop a Nespresso pod into the machine. As I wait for my coffee to brew, I spot the piece of paper tucked under a book on the kitchen island and pick it up, grinning at Indy's impeccable handwriting.

Thanks for last night. I had a lot of fun. Have a great day, Indy

Platonic. Sweet. That's what her note is. It's a thoughtful message to place me firmly in the friend zone after I spent hours tasting her sweet skin and making her shatter apart with her eyes squeezed tight, her back arched, and her hands clutching my bedsheets.

Jesus. Indy is sexy as hell. All the more so because she's sweet. And now, she's friend-zoning me for the first time in my life. The realization makes me laugh and I pick up my phone to message Austin for Indy's phone number.

No way am I letting her just slip away with the morning light after last night happened. Even though I'm not going to date her, even though there's no future for us, we need to at least talk about what went down. Clear the air. Make sure things aren't awkward at future Merrick family gatherings.

I tap out a text to Austin and send it just before my phone rings.

Slipping onto a barstool, I grip my coffee mug and answer.

"East?" Apprehension and hope swirl in my stomach. It's the first time my brother's contacted me since he entered rehab a week ago.

"Hey Noah," my brother's calm and measured voice comes through the line and I relax some just hearing it.

"How're you doing?" I raise my coffee to my mouth and take a swig. The hot brew along with Easton's voice dulls some of my headache.

"I'm okay," East sighs. "Fuck man, last week was fucking brutal but I feel good. For real this time, I've got my head on straight."

"That's good, man. I'm glad to hear it. Just focus on your recovery."

"That's it. I'm locked in, taking things day by day. But when I get out of here, I'm ready to get back on the ice. It's the only thing getting me through."

I tamp down the flicker of hope that spurs in my chest at his words. I know better than to believe them. I'm not saying that East doesn't mean them because right now, in this moment, he does. His voice is strong, his mind is clear, and a skate would do him good.

But when the temptations of the hockey world wave in front of his eyes, will he be able to choose hockey, choose our team, over a bottle of whiskey?

"You've got eleven weeks left," I point out. "Just take it one day at a time."

"But I feel great, Noah. Better than I've felt in a really long time."

"That's awesome, man. You're doing really good and I'm proud of you for reaching out and getting help."

He makes a weird sound, a cross between a snort and a

chuckle. East and I are as close as brothers can be but we don't do this shit. Talk about our feelings so openly. We were taught to keep our expressions blank and our mouths shut. Maybe that's why our family is so dysfunctional?

"Eleven weeks is a long time. I was tossing around the idea of just thirty days," he says after a moment. "Or sixty."

Some of the hope in my chest sinks. "Nah, stick it out, man. Give yourself this time to work through things and—"

"There's nothing to work through, Noah. This time, I swear it, I'm straight. I know all the reasons, all the mistakes, that landed me here and I'm not going to make them again."

"Take the extra time," I bite out. East and I have been down this road before, several times in fact. If he has any chance of sticking to his recovery, he needs to follow the process he committed to from the start.

I feel his frustration roll through the line but he doesn't say anything and I don't push it.

"What'd you do this weekend?" he asks, steering the conversation to calmer waters.

"Hung out with the team last night. We start training for the season opener on Monday."

Easton sighs, "Fuck, now I'm jealous."

"Don't be. We need you when we're closer to playing in the Finals."

"Yeah. How are the guys doing?"

"Everyone's good. Asking about you. Coach is going to fill them in this week."

"But I'm still good, right? I'll still be able to play."

I close my eyes, not sure how much information to divulge to my brother when he's already handling so much mentally. East and I have always played hockey together; we've always been viewed as a package deal. In many ways, my presence cushions his relationship with management and my performance on the ice softens his mistakes off of it. "Yeah, man. You're still good. We need you back so go all in these next few months and keep your head up." It's the truth, management hasn't said anything about replacing my brother. But how many chances will Easton get until his addiction is too much of a drain on a professional hockey team? The Hawks' owner, Scott Relend, needs to know his players are committed to the game, to the team, and will put that commitment over everything.

Easton's quiet on the line and I know his mind is processing, turning over my words, trying to read between the lines.

To distract him, I blurt out, "Indy's here."

"Indy?"

"Austin's cousin."

"Merrick?"

"That's the one."

"Oh yeah, she moved to Boston months ago. You didn't know that?"

"I think I'm the only person who didn't."

Easton snickers. "Dude, you have been fucked up since Courtney. Drunker than me half the time. No offense."

"None taken."

"Austin threw a little thing for her when she first got into town. Oh, I think it was the weekend you and Courtney sold your place. But anyway, it was a nice dinner with a lot of Vanny's and Claire's friends. It was a way to welcome her to the city."

I wrack my mind to recall the dinner he's talking about and something vague clicks. Shame fills my throat that I was so gutted and angry over Courtney that I literally tuned out everyone else's lives. Maybe if I had been more aware of what was going on months ago, my little brother wouldn't be in rehab now.

"How's she doing?" East asks after a second.

"Yeah, she's good. Really great. Loves the city, loves her work."

"That's right. She's a professor, isn't she?"

"She is."

Silence stretches for a long beat before Easton's laughter pulls me from my thoughts about Indy. "What's so funny?" I ask.

"Holy shit, Noah. Tell me you're not trying to get into Indiana Merrick's pants?"

"What?" I clear my throat, yanking on the back of my neck. "Of course not. I'm—"

"Fuuuuuck," Easton cuts me off. "You already did. Damn, man. Little Indy Merrick?" He fucking laughs. "This just made my fucking day. My week! Thank you."

"East, it's not like that."

"Yeah? What's it like?"

"Indy's a great girl. A cool girl. She's…"

"Gorgeous." My brother fills in the blank.

I blow out an exhale, making a sound of agreement.

"Why are you acting so weird? Indy's awesome. When did it go down?"

"Last night," I blurt out, regretting telling Easton the moment I do. This isn't the topic that should be discussed on Easton's first call home. "I'm sorry. This isn't important. We should be talking about—"

"This," my brother interrupts. "Seriously, I'm relieved to call you and talk about something that isn't alcohol- or recovery-related. Just connect with the world again and be part of a conversation that doesn't delve into my hidden feelings or triggers."

I let out a breath. "Okay."

"So you fucked Indy?"

I wince. "We slept together."

Easton laughs. "Shit, man. You *like* her."

I don't say anything, not wanting to agree with or deny his correct observation.

"So?" he presses.

"So nothing. Man, she's Austin's cousin. She's Jeremiah's daughter. She's wifey material. A good girl, a smart girl, a way-out-of-my-league girl. I can't just hook up with Indy. She's the kind of girl you go all in with or not at all."

"But you slept with her."

"I shouldn't have," I groan, knowing that tangling Indy up in my sheets and devouring her was fucked up on my part. Still, not regretting it one bit.

"She tell you that?" My brother sounds skeptical.

"No."

"So? Why are you jumping to conclusions?"

"It just, it doesn't seem right. She's not a puck bunny."

"Definitely not a puck bunny. But maybe someone you could think about hanging out with, casually date. You don't have to put a ring on it to make it meaningful."

I take another swig of coffee, knowing that on some level my brother is offering a very rational point of view. But it doesn't feel rational. It feels like if I dated Indy, it would entail more than I can give. More than I'm good for. And it's stupid but I don't want that for her. I want more for her than me. "Not gonna happen, man. I just need to have a conversation with her, make sure we're good and on the same page, and forget last night ever happened."

"Did you kiss her in public last night? At the team thing?" Easton wonders, probably imagining me sucking face with Indy as the team looks on. Like I have been with other girls ever since Courtney called off our wedding.

"No, it wasn't like that. She came home with me."

"Just out of the blue?"

I swear. "I'm not explaining this well. Last night, the team got together. Claire and Indy showed up and Claire"—I wince, not wanting to bring up alcohol but at the same time, not knowing how to avoid it—"well, she had a little too much to drink. Austin took her home and asked me to keep an eye on Indy."

"I doubt he meant *sleep with my cousin*," Easton supplies but his words are wrapped in humor, which encourages me to continue with the story.

"Smartass. Torsten got involved—"

"Shots," Easton surmises.

"Anyway, on the way to her house there was an accident and traffic was backed up so I invited her here. I swear I wasn't planning on doing anything but then…"

"You fucked her."

"We slept together," I amend. "She was gone before I even woke up."

"Ouch. Color me impressed." Easton snorts.

I laugh. "I can't believe we are having this long of a conversation about a hook-up."

"Nah, it's because you like her, man."

"It's not going to happen," I reiterate.

"Yeah, okay." He chuckles. "Hey, how's Claire?"

I frown. "She's good. You gonna ask about Austin next?"

"Nah. I'll still see his ugly mug. I've been cleared to have visitors so he's coming next week."

"Count me in too."

"Yeah?"

"Of course, East. I want to support you through this. Whatever you need."

Easton clears his throat. "Thanks, Noah."

"It's only eleven weeks. Stick it out. Austin and I will drop by next week. We'll have lunch."

"Yeah, okay," my brother sighs, and I can hear the thread of uncertainty in the sound. He's struggling. For all his talk about being straight, Easton battles a lot of demons. He puts up one hell of a fight, but sometimes, there are just too many for one man to slay.

"Hang in there," I say.

"You too, Noah. And honestly man, if you're feeling Indy, give it a shot."

"We'll see," I say noncommittally. "Later, East."

"Bye, bro." He hangs up.

Draining my coffee mug, I stand from the barstool and stretch. I rinse my mug out in the sink and place it next to Indy's. Checking my phone, I note it's already ten and Austin replied to my text.

Austin: 555-9317 All okay with Indy?

Me: Yeah man, just wanted to check in on her.

Austin: ???

Me: There was crazy traffic getting to her place last night so she crashed here. She was gone when I woke up and just wanted to make sure she's good.

Austin: Ah, got it. Thanks for looking out and keeping an eye on Indy. She doesn't normally do the club scene and I didn't want to leave her.

A ripple of guilt swirls through me. Shit. Austin thinks I'm looking out for Indy and I am…but the elephant in the room grows larger.

Me: No worries. All good. Lunch next week with East?

Austin: Name the day.

I shift my weight from foot to foot, wondering if I should call Indy or forget about it. In the end, my curiosity and Easton's words win out and I hit send.

7

INDY

"You had sex with him?!" Claire's eyes are so wide, they may fall right out of their sockets.

I nod, an uncertain smile locked on my face.

"Like 'we-drank-tequila-and-now-we're-blowing-off-some-steam' sex or 'I'm-ripping-your-clothes-from-your-body-and-having-my-way-with-you' sex?"

I wrinkle my nose. "Somewhere in the middle, I'd guess."

"You'd guess?"

I roll my eyes. "I'd say."

Claire's mouth drops open and her eyes grow even larger. How is that possible? "Holy hell! I'm so glad I got blitzed and left you behind now."

I snort, shaking my head. "You kind of suck."

"I'm kind of awesome," she refutes, taking a swig of her Diet Coke. "Want one?"

"It's ten a.m."

"It's hangover gold."

My temples throb. "Okay, I'll take one."

She reaches into the mini fridge in her bedroom and tosses me a can.

"I can't believe you set up your mini fridge from college in your childhood bedroom." I pop the tab and take a sip. The bubbles are surprisingly soothing.

"I can't believe I moved home after college at all," Claire laments.

"It's a tough market right now."

"It's always a tough market. It's good, isn't it?" She waggles her eyebrows as I drink more Diet Coke.

"On this one thing, you may be right."

Claire grins. "Okay, tell me more."

"There's nothing to tell. We hooked up, I fell asleep—"

"In his bed."

"Yes, in his bed. Then, I woke up and left."

She gasps. "You ghosted him?"

I roll my eyes. "Claire, it's not like that. It was one drunken night that meant—" The shrill ringing of my cell phone cuts through the air and I glance at it, frowning at the unknown number.

"Gonna get that?" my cousin prods, way too excited for someone who drank their body weight in vodka last night.

I swipe right. "Hello?"

"Indy? Hey, it's Noah."

Oh. My. God. Noah Scotch is calling me?

"Hey Noah. Uh, how are you?"

At my words, Claire's mouth falls open and she stands from the bed, jumping up and down like a game show contestant who just won a trip to Aruba. I swat at her.

Noah chuckles through the line and it sounds nervous. Unsteady. It makes me smile. "Good. I'm good. I was actually calling to check on you."

"Me? I'm good too."

Why are you having the most awkward conversation

ever? Claire holds up a ripped-out piece of notebook paper with the words scrawled across it.

I flip her off and she snorts, resuming her scribbling.

"I got worried when you were already gone this morning."

I wince. "Oh. Well, I just didn't want to be a bother. I really appreciate your letting me crash last night."

"You're not a bother and it's not a big deal. Anytime."

"Well, thank you. I had fun last night."

"Me too. You made it a hell of a lot more interesting than usual."

I laugh and Noah joins in. "It surprised me too," I admit.

"Yeah," Noah agrees. "But…we're cool right?"

"Yep. Very cool," I say quickly and Claire winces.

"Good," Noah says, his voice normal. "I'm glad you were there last night, Indy. I feel like a huge douche for not knowing you moved to Boston. Even Easton made fun of me."

"You talked to Easton?"

At that, Claire stops writing and looks up, her face stricken and her eyes burning with curiosity. I hold up a finger.

"He called me this morning. He's doing pretty well. Made it through the withdrawal part and is taking things day by day. Austin and I are going to have lunch with him one day next week."

"Wow. That's great. I mean, I'm glad to hear he's doing well."

Claire relaxes slightly but crawls back onto the bed and sits beside me, elbowing me until our heads are touching and she's joined my conversation with Noah.

"Yeah. Me too."

Noah clears his throat. "Anyway, I just wanted to make

sure you're okay and that things between us aren't going to be awkward."

"Not awkward at all." My voice comes out two octaves higher than normal and Claire looks at me like I'm an alien.

I stick my tongue out at her but she just shakes her head at me.

"Good. Well, thanks again for last night. I really had a good time."

"Me too," I say, blushing as Claire rolls her eyes. "Anyway, I got to go but thanks for checking in on me."

"Of course. Take care."

"You too. Bye." I hang up and round on Claire.

"You are so fucking lame." She hits me in the head with a pillow.

"What did you want me to say?"

"You friend-zoned him."

"That's where he belongs. In my friend zone."

Claire shakes her head. "Indy, you're into him," she shrieks, dancing out of my reach as I lunge at her.

"I am not."

"You totally are. I could tell by your conversation."

I laugh. "No way. You kept distracting me."

"Uh, I think you meant Noah kept distracting you." She wiggles her eyebrows.

I groan, flinging myself back onto her bed.

"You're into him," she tells me cheerily, smiling like she won the freaking lottery.

"There is something wrong with you."

"Because I'm happy that you finally have the hots for a guy who knows how to use them to *your* advantage. See what I did there? Your advantage, Indy. Jesus, if the rumors are true…just tell me, how many orgasms?"

"Claire!" I blush, feeling it to the tips of my ears.

"Oh my God! That many?" She drops next to me on her bed. "I'm so jealous."

I drop a pillow over her face. Still, I hear her muffled laughter.

Removing the pillow, I narrow my eyes at her. "It was a one-night thing. It's over. I'm not going to hook up with Noah Scotch again."

My cousin snickers, shaking her head at me. "Yeah right. We'll see about that."

I TOTALLY WANT to hook up with Noah Scotch again.

I hate Claire for even putting the thought into my head.

Normal Indy, smart, determined, focused workaholic, would never consider such allusions. Now that the night has come and gone, I find myself second-guessing if he looked at me with desire or pity.

Was it heat in his eyes? Or my own hope placing it there?

Did he bring me back to his place because he wanted me there? Or because he was too exhausted to wait out the traffic?

But then why did he call…?

That's the thought that buzzes in my mind, keeping me warm and fuzzy about Noah Scotch when I would normally dismiss the entire encounter as a fun, thrilling, drunken night I know better than to repeat.

After drinking a much-needed coffee to clear my head, I left Noah's apartment and went straight to my aunt and uncle's house. When Aunt Mary spotted me letting myself in at six this morning, she pulled the door wide open and handed me a fresh mug of hot coffee.

"I'm not even going to ask," she said before I could

explain rocking Claire's skintight dress and holding the heels in my hand even though my feet were freezing standing on her porch so early in the morning. "Come on in and put on a sweatshirt before you catch a cold."

"Thanks, Auntie." I kissed her hello and scurried to the living room where she passed me a sweatshirt and covered me in a warm blanket.

Four sips of coffee in and I was snoozing on the couch, knowing Claire would wake me up when she finally dragged her hungover ass from bed.

While I should have just gone home to my place, I didn't want to be alone this morning. That too is out of the ordinary for me. But after a night wrapped in Noah's arms, his scent, in his freaking bed, I needed to seek out my cousin as if my self-preservation depended on it.

Maybe it's because deep down I knew Claire would plant ideas in my head. Ideas I want to consider but don't want to admit.

Gah. I'm a mess.

But spending the day with Claire, watching movies and nursing our hangovers, was fun. It was reminiscent of my college years but in the comfort of her parents' home instead of a stinky dorm.

Uncle Joe made us panini sandwiches for lunch and Aunt Mary kept us hydrated with water and Gatorade. While I know it's a little ridiculous that we holed up here instead of my place, I think Aunt Mary and Uncle Joe like being "in the know" about our lives. Especially since Vanny is now married and Austin's on the road so much.

With Claire and now me being back in Boston, my aunt and uncle as well as my parents have regressed into helicopter parenting. I may complain about it all day, every day but not when I'm hungover and out of sorts and wanting to have someone make me lunch and bring me coffee.

Alas, by dusk, I force myself to leave Claire's side and head home, this time clad in her sweatpants and a hoodie, a ratty pair of Claire's Uggs on my feet. Once I enter my apartment, I flip on the lights and throw myself into the shower. Heat and steam make me feel like myself again. Once I no longer smell like sugary sweet vodka cocktails, I step out of the shower and shrug into a robe, wrapping my hair in a towel. I brew a cup of tea and sit down at my kitchen table, flipping open my laptop.

Then, I throw myself into my work. I'm organizing a student research trip to Bangladesh over winter break. The trip will foster my own research on microfinance loans and the role of women in a patriarchal society while also exposing my students to conducting field research.

A strange sense of excitement rolls through me as I fill a spreadsheet with logistical information. It feels like my entire outlook has shifted in the past twenty-four hours. Somewhere in between watching Claire get ready for the night and now, I've decided that I'm tired of just being Indiana "checks-all-the-boxes,   does-all-the-right-things-in-the-right-order" Merrick.

I don't want to hide behind my laptop and inside my cozy apartment when my cousins are out in the city, meeting people and mingling.

Flirting with Noah, noting the way his lips turned up as if they were grinning of their own accord when I spoke, and the way his eyes shone as they peered into mine was intoxicating. Joking around with Torsten and Panda smudged the lines around my insecurities until I felt accepted, a part of the group sitting around the bar last night, taking shots. Going home with Noah and waking up this morning, sore from delicious sex, and hungover from a night filled with fun, was eye-opening. Exhilarating. Exciting with a ton of possible outcomes I don't know the answers to.

Chewing the corner of my lip, I take a sip of my tea and lean back in my chair. Why can't I be an impactful professor *and* have a full social calendar? Why can't I conduct research, write articles, publish, *and* do drinks in the city followed by hot sex?

As the realization that I'm an adult, capable of making choices and decisions about my life, sinks in, I grin. For the first time ever, I have a salary. I have my dream job. I have a full, blank canvas ahead of me, waiting to be painted. Don't I want to decorate it with as much color, as many experiences, as possible?

Hell yeah, I do.

I open a new tab on my browser. The cursor blinks in the search engine as I type the name Noah Scotch.

When the page populates, a thrill rushes down my spine. Sure, there are photos of Noah with Courtney and other gorgeous women. But in all of them, his smile is the same. He's still the nice guy from my teenage years. He's still someone I can trust and have some fun with.

So, what's stopping us from having a little fun while we both focus on our dream careers?

By the time I crawl into bed, it's after midnight but I'm not tired.

For the first time in years, my future looks like a question mark.

And I've never been so excited for the unknown that awaits.

8

NOAH

The team isn't gelling the way we should, especially not before our season opener. With East in rehab, a new guy, Sims, is filling in for him.

Austin, Easton, and I have played hockey together for so many years that our performance on the ice is natural. It's so effortless that sometimes, I don't have to think about it. I know that when I hit the puck to the right, my brother will be there. I know, without looking, that Austin has my back. Our rhythm has been honed from years of practice and hundreds of games working out kinks and improving.

With Sims, our grace is nonexistent, messing up our entire offensive line.

"Come on!" Austin hollers, aggravated when Sims misses the puck and gets slammed into the boards.

Sims shakes his head, skating away to pull himself together.

We've been at it all week, grueling practices that end with the entire team pissed off. Part of me feels for Sims. It isn't easy filling Easton's skates and being on the receiving end of Austin's frustration. But another part of me can't worry too much. It's messed up but I don't want Sims to settle in too easily. In ten weeks, my brother will be back and I want his position to still be his when he's out of rehab.

"Again!" Austin shouts and the team resumes our positions.

We run through the drill three more times until Coach Phillips calls practice. The energy in the locker room is depleted, team morale at an all-time low. I take a shower and dress quickly, just wanting to get out of the arena and put this shitty practice behind me.

"Hey." Torsten appears at my side as I close my locker door.

"What's up?" I ask.

He shrugs. "Want to grab lunch?"

"Yeah, sure," I agree, my stomach growling. As much as I want to get out of the arena, I don't really want to go home to my empty space and dwell on the season.

Torsten shoulders his practice bag and I follow him out of the arena, sliding into the passenger seat of his car.

"What are you in the mood for?" he asks.

"I haven't had Mexican in ages," I say after a moment. My stomach rumbles loudly at the suggestion.

"I know a place," Torsten says, pulling out of the arena and onto the road. He blows out a long sigh. "Today was rough."

"Tell me about it. Sims is never where he's supposed to be."

Torsten grips the top of the steering wheel, glancing at me. "You think East will be ready to play in a few months?" His tone is measured but I hear the uncertainty, the skepticism, underlining his words.

I blow out a breath and gaze out the window. I want my brother to claim the ice in a little over two months and

remind everyone, the team, management, fans across Mass-
achusetts and the entire country, that he's a fucking god on
the ice.

But the reality of the situation is that it's not going to
happen. Even if East was in the best shape of his life before
rehab, which he wasn't, he's certainly going to take a few
weeks to find his rhythm again. In the interim, Sims is our
best option and everyone is giving him shit. If we don't start
the season strong, it will be tough to change morale and rally
for a spot in the play-offs. "I don't know, man."

Torsten's silent for a few moments. "My contract is up at
the end of the season," he says quietly.

I turn and frown at him. "And?"

"And, if the Hawks don't re-sign me or trade me—"

"Why wouldn't they re-sign you?"

He chuckles but it's humorless. "Scotch, I'm nearly
thirty-eight years old. The team just called up two rookies. I
might not be starting by the end of this season and I know it."

I hold up a hand, about to refute him, but at the glint in
his eyes, I swallow back my words. Torsten has been a
cornerstone of the Hawks Franchise for so long, it's hard to
imagine him not playing for the team. It's even harder to
fathom him not playing hockey at all.

"I need this season to be spectacular. I need to perform
the best I possibly can every shot I have on the ice. I need this
to be our year, to win the Cup. Maybe because it will be my
last. But also because it's my best chance at being re-signed.
If I'm not…"

"What?" I ask, frowning. What the hell is Torsten trying
to say?

He gives me a look, amusement flaring in his eyes for a
second. "I won't have a visa. I'll need to head home to
Norway."

I swear, staring at my teammate, my friend, for a long minute.

He turns his gaze back to the road but I continue to process the bomb he just dropped in my lap. Of course I knew Torsten was from Norway, but I never thought about how he lives in the US. I never realized that without hockey, his entire life here wouldn't be possible.

Torsten Hansen has been in the US since he was nineteen years old. He has investments here, his life is here. What the hell would he even do in Norway to start over at almost forty? I shake my head, pinching the bridge of my nose.

First, we may lose Easton. Our other defenseman, James Ryan, has been mentally absent since his wife passed. Now, Torsten brings up this.

What the hell is happening to my team? How are we going to compete this year with all of our top players, the seasoned guys who know the rhythm, who understand the flow, being pushed to the fringes?

I fix him with a hard stare. "Then we make this our best season."

Torsten laughs but by the expression that crosses his face, I know he's worried. Worried and hopeful.

"I'm serious," I repeat.

He nods, shooting me a sympathetic look. "And if East can't get it together?"

I blow out a breath, knowing what he's asking of me, even if it's indirectly. "Then I'll get Sims up to speed. I'll make sure he's ready. Austin will too." Fucking hell though. I don't want to help East's competition when my loyalty, on every level, belongs to my brother.

But can I watch Torsten leave the team, leave the country, because Easton made a series of choices that landed him back in rehab?

Stuck between a rock and a hard place, I shake my head and turn to look back out the window. Torsten and I, lost in our own thoughts, remain silent until we pull up to a tiny but brightly decorated restaurant in Boston's West End.

"What is this place?" I ask, sliding out of the car.

Torsten glances at me over the hood. "A hidden gem."

I snort, following him into the small restaurant. The moment I enter, the delicious scent of culinary expertise wraps around me and I breathe in deeply.

Torsten chuckles and tips his chin toward a table.

I follow him, glancing at the plates on other patrons' tables. Everything looks delicious. Bright, colorful, classic Mexican dishes with modern twists.

Is that sushi on nachos? This place *is* a hidden gem.

Right before I slide onto a chair, I glance up and my gaze connects with Little Indy Merrick. Thoughts of our night together flicker through my mind and instead of feeling awkward, like I should get the hell out of here before she latches onto me, the way I would with other women, I grin.

She freezes, like a deer caught in headlights, her fingers hovering over the keyboard of her laptop.

Some of the tension in my shoulders deflates just seeing her again. "Indy!" I call out to her.

Across from me, Torsten turns in his chair. "Hey there, sweetheart. Want to join us for lunch?"

Indy stares, her eyes widening like she can't believe we're here. Her hair is twisted into a complicated-looking knot on the top of her head. Big, triangle earrings dangle from her ears. She's rocking this tie-dye sweater that looks more like a throwback to the nineties than what's trending today. The sleeves are pushed up on her arms. Other girls would look ridiculous but on Indy, the look just…works. She looks comfortable and cute and completely confident in her ensemble from way back when.

She stares for so long that I wonder if she's feeling that awkward need to run, or if she's worried that I'll somehow latch onto her, or if I interrupted something important for her work by greeting her.

She shakes her head, moving to tuck a strand of hair behind her ear before realizing it's tied up. A blush works over her cheeks and she ducks her head, offering a small smile that I can't help but return. She's adorable when she's flustered.

"Hi, guys. Sure, thanks." She closes her laptop, slips it into her bag, and picks up the coffee she's drinking.

I pull up a third chair to our table and Indy sits down, dropping her bag onto the back of the chair.

Torsten dips his head forward to kiss her cheek hello and I roll my eyes even though I know he means nothing by it. It's how he greets every woman, from the college girls who beg for his autograph to the grandmas who tell him about their hockey-playing grandkids. Still, the flicker of irritation that buzzes through me at his greeting Indy is new. I shake it off.

"What are you guys doing here?" she asks, her gaze darting between Torsten and me.

"Are you kidding?" Torsten replies. "This place has some of the best food I've ever had."

"I know, right?" she agrees. "It's one of my faves. I live just around the corner and I'm trying to guard it with my life. The last thing we need is its reputation getting out and the place being overrun with tourists."

"It's Scotch's first time here. Don't hate me for bringing him along," Torsten teases.

Indy grins and tips her head toward me. "Just this one

pass." She raises a finger to Torsten before glancing at me. "You're going to love it."

"I bet," I agree. "What did you order?"

"Oh, I haven't ordered yet. Just a coffee." Indy lifts her cup to her lips and takes a sip, her eyes distracted again.

"Hungry?" Torsten asks.

She nods. "Starving. I can't even believe the time. I was so lost in my work."

"What are you working on?" I ask, leaning back in my chair.

Her expression transforms, her face opening like a sunflower. Her eyes dazzle and I find myself mesmerized by the way she glows. "Oh, gosh, I'm so excited about it!" She chuckles, ducking her head and nudging a menu in my direction. "Let's order first."

Torsten grabs a menu. "Just building that anticipation, huh, Indy?"

She flushes, her cheeks turning redder. She wrinkles her nose. "It's probably not going to seem so exciting to you guys. You're going to think I'm lame."

"Nah, can't be lamer than overanalyzing hockey plays." I drop my menu. "Order for me. Whatever your favorite dish is."

Her eyes meet mine. Deep green and bottomless, like the sea. Jesus, a man could get lost in Indy's eyes. "Okay."

When our server, Shell, arrives, Indy orders for us and Torsten tacks on his lunch and a couple appetizers to split. Then, we turn our attention toward Indy.

Her grin is straight up goofy, like she can't hold her news in one second longer. "I'm planning a trip!"

"A trip?" Torsten asks, frowning as he tries to piece together why this is news at all.

"Yes!" Indy exclaims. "A research trip. I'm going to take

a group of my second-year students to Bangladesh over winter break. We're going to be learning about microfinance initiatives that favor women and how this lends to household social mobility. It's statistically proven that women make better decisions for the family than men, which is one of the reasons why these loans, although small, have been so impactful."

"Wow," I mutter, impressed.

Torsten's eyes are wide as he stares at Indy like he doesn't know her.

She chuckles and bites the corner of her mouth. "Lame?"

"Not at all, Indy. That's... pretty fucking awesome." I like the concept of her research trip almost as much as I like hearing her talk about it.

"You're a badass brainiac, aren't you?" Torsten asks. "You must be bored out of your mind at hockey games."

"Nah." She shakes her head.

"She doesn't watch them. She's too busy reading her books," I explain to Torsten who laughs as Indy blushes and averts her gaze.

"The trip is in December?" I ask as the server drops off our appetizers.

"Yes. I've got so much planning and organizing to do before then. I need to choose the students in the next week or so too. Lots to do but I'm really excited about it. I remember my first time conducting field research. There's nothing like it. Being connected to strangers, working toward a common goal, feeling like you're contributing to a big change for someone's life. This is the reason why I wanted to become a professor. I never anticipated having this opportunity my first year but the professor who usually runs the trip has a medical issue and backed out." She talks using her hands, gesturing wildly. It's something she does when she's excited and I like that she's passionate about her work. Her eyes twinkle as she says, "Lucky me."

"I'm sure you'll figure it all out," Torsten says.

"Hope so." Indy picks up a bowl and adds some salad to her place. "How was practice?"

Torsten and I both groan.

"That good, huh?"

9

INDY

They grimace.

Immediately, I feel bad for Noah and Torsten. It's hard when you've been playing with the same guys for so many years. Noah, Austin, and Easton have comprised the first-string offensive line for over four years. The guys have been playing together since they were kids. Having someone new trying to fall into their rhythm is a huge change for everyone, including the new guy.

"I'm sorry, guys. I remember when my dad—"

"Had to team up with Ray Silver." Torsten leans back in his chair. "They ended up being unstoppable."

"They did." I tip my coffee mug in his direction, pleased he already got my point. "I can't imagine how difficult this is for you guys. Or for the new guy."

"Eddie Sims," Noah supplies.

"Sims." I nod, committing his name to my memory. "It's frustrating and it's going to be a lot of baby steps. But you all have to be open-minded and willing to change certain things. It could lead to an even better performance." I duck my head and bite my tongue. Why am I preaching to these guys? After a tough morning on the ice, it's probably the last thing they need. "Sorry."

"No," Noah exhales, scrubbing a hand along his jawline. "You're right. I just hate hearing the truth sometimes."

Torsten snorts. "It's hard because we want East back."

"Of course you do," I sympathize, glancing at Noah. His expression is severe, the lines around his eyes deeper than they were a moment ago. I can't imagine how he must be feeling right now. Most likely pinging between loyalty to his brother and loyalty to his team.

Torsten's phone rings and he pulls it from his pocket, his scowl intensifying as he swears. "I'm sorry, guys, I need to take this. Give me a minute?" He glances from me to Noah.

I nod as Noah waves him away. Torsten stands and lifts the phone to his ear, heading for the exit.

When Noah looks at me, I catch his gaze and hold it. His eyes burn, darker than midnight. I can't read any of his thoughts and a thrill dances through my body. "Getting Sims up to the task isn't a betrayal of Easton," I say slowly. "You know that, right?"

He exhales heavily and nods.

I'm thankful more appetizers arrive at this moment.

"I've never had sushi nachos." I change the subject.

"Me neither. Especially with this Tex-Mex twist." Noah adds some nachos covered with hot peppers, raw tuna, and a sriracha-based sauce on my plate. He bites into a nacho and moans. "These are surprisingly delicious." He nudges my plate toward me and I take a bite.

"Everything here is," I agree.

Torsten reappears, looking distracted and overwhelmed. "Noah, man, I'm so sorry. I need to go. Something came up. Do you want to come with me or—"

"No worries, man. I'll catch an Uber or something. Here, take some food to go." Noah waves to a server.

Torsten shakes his head. "It's okay. I'm really in a rush. See you guys later?"

"See you, Torsten." I wave, wondering what could have pulled him away so suddenly. "I hope nothing's wrong," I say to Noah as we watch Torsten leave the restaurant.

He frowns, chewing his lip thoughtfully but doesn't offer any insight on the issue. Noah picks up another nacho and pops it into his mouth. "I get what you said about not betraying my brother but it feels…" he pauses, circling back to our earlier conversation. "Messed up somehow. Today was just, it was pretty fucking bad."

"I'm sorry." I remember the rough patches my dad went through when he played. Some days, no matter how hard the team practiced, the rhythm just wasn't there. If it kept up for more than a week, the frustration plunged him into a mood and he'd sport an expression similar to the grimace Noah's wearing now.

"I gotta work with the new kid, Sims. Part of it is the fact that he's not used to playing so hard, for so long at this level. But part of it is the rest of us. We're not making it easy for him either."

"Because of Easton?" I guess.

Noah nods. "It sucks. East's my brother and I'd do anything for him. We've always kind of come as a duo. We've played together our whole lives. But the team is important too. I don't want to compromise our being ready for the opening game because I'm not willing to make sure we're where we need to be."

"Don't you think if you come right out and explain that to Easton, he would understand?"

"I think he'd feel betrayed."

"Maybe," I say slowly, turning the situation over in my mind. "Or maybe he'd feel a little relieved that there isn't all this pressure waiting to hit him in the face the second he leaves rehab. Like, now you're out so get your skates on and deliver the Cup."

Noah purses his lips. "I never thought about it like that. I mean, hockey is his life. Same as me. He can't wait to be back out on the ice with his stick in hand."

"That may be true. But that doesn't mean there isn't any anxiety or pressure associated with it either. How would you feel? If you were in East's position right now?"

He's quiet for a long moment, thinking over my question. "I wouldn't want to let the team down."

"Exactly. Maybe if the team is performing well, it's less pressure on Easton too. Less of a need for him to come back and be a superstar right out of the gate. His recovery is a life-long journey. He's going to have hiccups and tough days. The most important thing he can do is manage his stress, know what his capabilities are, and settle into a routine."

"But what if he loses his spot?" Noah cringes, as if the thought alone is painful.

"What if he doesn't and takes the ice when he's truly ready to perform?" I counter. "You just don't know, Noah. But you have to do what's best for Easton and what's best for the team. You're thinking of this as an if/or scenario but really it may just be a both."

He chews another nacho, nodding slowly. Then he turns toward me and his shoulders drop, relief filling his features. "I think you may be right, Indy."

I pat his hand and eat another nacho.

"You can bill me by the hour," he adds and we both laugh.

"Listen, Indy," Noah starts and I know exactly what's coming.

I've spent the past few days remembering everything about last weekend. The way Noah's hands felt on my skin, the tickle of his breath on the back of my neck, how his abs rippled—yes, rippled—when he pushed inside of me.

My face heats at the reminder and I hold up a hand. "It's cool, Noah."

He shakes his head. "We can't just pretend it never happened."

"Why?" I blurt out, smacking a hand over my mouth.

Noah chuckles but I don't miss the way his eyes narrow and his jawline tightens. "Because, Little Indy, you're not just some chick I'll never see again. I care about your family and I care about you and I don't want things to be weird."

I shake my head. "They won't be. Look, wasn't today nice? This, it's fun."

He groans, running a hand along the edge of his jaw. It could cut freaking steel and I zero in on the movement. "That's another part of the problem."

"What is?" What are we even talking about? Maybe Claire was right. Noah is distracting.

"I like hanging out with you."

I beam. Like shoot rainbows and unicorns from eyes type of beaming. "You do?"

His brow furrows and he nods.

My beaming intensifies, as much as it's possible. "I like hanging with you too. To be honest, you're the first guy in a long time I feel normal around. Not counting my best friend from home."

"Normal?"

"Yeah. Like I can be my nerdy, type A self around."

He snorts. "You're not nerdy, Indy."

"You don't know me that well, then."

"You're the fucking cutest." He chuckles, his expression

softening. "Everyone should have some of your sunshine in their lives."

I freeze at the sincerity in his tone even as my mind trips over itself in glee at his words. *Everyone should have some of your sunshine in their lives.* Jesus. What kind of man says things like that to a woman after one night together?

Noah swallows, shaking his head in amusement. "I was thinking…"

I raise an eyebrow, my heart rate ticking up.

"Since we like hanging together and we have such an easy connection, what if we…were friends."

"Just friends?" I ask, disappointment streaking through me. That's the scary thing. How am I disappointed about being friends with this beautiful man when I should be grateful? Or even relieved?

Noah nods. "Can't give you any more of a commitment than that, Indy. I'm not the serious commitment, marrying, a houseful of babies kind of guy. Not anymore. Hell, I'm not even the dog kind of guy. The most long-term commitment I've had is to my goldfish Dorothy."

I crack a smile, knowing he's trying to be upfront with me. Honest. Still, his words sting and scrape even though they're what I should want to hear. They're the rational option. "I get it. It's better this way. I don't date—"

"Hockey players," he finishes, biting his lip.

"Right," I agree.

"So no awkwardness."

"None at all."

"We can hang out?"

"Anytime," I quip, way more casual than I feel.

"Cool."

I grin but my chest sinks a little and I'm not sure what to make of that.

10

NOAH

Eating lunch with Indy is fun. It's not awkward, even though I saw her naked just last weekend. If anything, it's nice. Chill. The most fun I've had sharing a meal with a woman in a long time.

It seems most things with Indy are effortless and casual and lacking the expectations usually associated with my interactions with females. After a tough few days, her presence is soothing.

"You live around here?" I ask as I settle the bill. Indy tries one more time to slip money across the table at me but I ignore it, shaking my head as I sign the credit card slip.

"Just around the corner," she says, tucking her folded notes back into her purse. "Thanks for lunch."

"Thanks for eating with me. If you weren't here, I would have ended up eating alone." I give her my best sad puppy-dog eyes and she snorts.

"Yeah for like three seconds until any of your admiring fans ambushed you."

I chuckle, glancing around and noting several extra-long glances in our direction. "Well, if you're just around the corner, I can help you carry some of these takeout boxes home."

"What? I can't take all these," she says, her eyes wide as they take in the five boxes.

It's typical of Torsten to order half the menu but he usually sticks around to inhale it all. Something is going on with him and by the hints he dropped about his visa on the way here, I'm more than concerned.

"Of course you can. You'll be organizing this big student trip all week and need breaks to eat."

"Sushi nachos?" She raises an eyebrow.

I laugh. "No, we didn't box those. But you have chicken enchiladas and veggie fajitas. Come on." I stand up, stacking the boxes and picking them up.

Indy doesn't argue again. She just shoulders her bag with her laptop and picks up an appetizer of guacamole and chips and follows me into the autumn day.

"It's this way," she says and I fall in step beside her as we walk toward her place.

"This is convenient. Living so close to all these restaurants and shops." I scan the little market and coffee shop we walk past.

"I love living in the West End. Actually, I am obsessed with my place. Wait 'til you see it."

I glance at her, surprised by the statement. Indy seems a little removed from all the luxury and highbrow lifestyle that easily impressed Courtney. We round another corner and Indy walks faster, pointing to an old, lone building. "That's it," she squeaks.

The second I see her apartment building, I know immediately why she loves it so much.

"You live in a tenement building?" We cross the street.

"Not just any tenement building. The Last Tenement!

This is literally the last one standing even though these streets were once filled with them. The West End is rich with history, with the story of how many immigrant families got their start in Boston; it sucks that they knocked them all down."

I stop outside of Indy's door and stare up at the four-story apartment building. She's right, a throwback to an earlier time, it is an overlooked piece of history of Boston's West End tenements and immigrant roots. Indy's place sticks out like a sore thumb amid the newer high-rises and ongoing construction.

A billboard plasters one side of the lone apartment building advertising a new exhibit at the Museum of Science. Behind me, dust kicks up as construction rages on, and across the street, the rich sounds of a saxophone pierce the air, the musician lost to the music, his eyes closed.

This place is a hidden, glittering treasure in a sea of normal. "I can see why you love it so much," I tell her truthfully. Courtney would have scoffed if I ever proposed living in a place like this. Hell, I probably would have overlooked it too. But seeing the way Indy stares at her apartment building and sees beyond the old brick and narrow windows makes me realize just how much Courtney and I were missing.

I follow Indy inside. The apartment building, although clean and well-maintained, still holds on to the scent of a bygone era. Small black and white tiles cover the ground as refurbished mahogany curves over the entryway. Glancing up at the narrow stairs, I like that there isn't an elevator.

Accustomed to my teammates' and my luxury apartments, Indy's place is a reminder that sometimes, less is more. Steeped in history and simplicity, I feel welcomed before we even push into her apartment door on the second floor.

She holds her arms out wide, as if to show off her space.

Grinning at me, she announces, "I know it's not much, but it's home. Welcome."

The ceilings are low, the space is cramped, but stepping into her space is like diving into her personality. Neat bookshelves line the walls with artfully placed knickknacks serving as separators and bookends. A simple leather couch sits in the living room and the decorative pillows are all in varying shades of beige and tan with a throw tossed over the back. Artwork hangs on the walls in perfectly spaced frames. While her apartment is neat and orderly, it's welcoming. Her kitchen doubles as a workstation and I grin when I note her stacked piles of folders and notebooks as well as a little cup with pens and highlighters.

She shifts from one foot to the other before removing the takeout boxes from my hand and placing them on the kitchen counter. "Would you like a coffee?"

"Sure," I agree, not wanting to leave. "I like your place," I add truthfully, my gaze landing on the window that overlooks the street, allowing a beam of natural light to stream inside.

She gives me a disbelieving look.

"I'm serious," I say, gesturing to her living room. "You live in a living piece of history."

"That's my favorite part." She prepares her French press.

"There's something to be said for simplicity. For using the space you have," I tack on, suddenly very aware that my 2,000-square-foot-plus Beacon Hill brownstone is ridiculously wasteful for a bachelor who currently lives alone and spends weeks at a time not sleeping there.

"I couldn't believe it when it went on the market for rent," Indy says, her eyes dancing with excitement, like she's reliving the moment. "I know it's not glamorous. Or high-end. I know I could get something newer for the rent I pay here but I saw it and…" she trails off, shrugging. "I just fell in love. It's cozy. Feels like home."

I clear my throat. "That's more than I can say about my place."

She rolls her eyes. "Your place is gorgeous."

"Do your parents live close by?"

"Not too far. They're in Back Bay. Dad was mortified when he saw my little walk-up." She laughs and I can tell she's not even remotely offended by it. Passing me a coffee cup, she gestures that we can take a seat on the couch.

I drop into an easy chair and she sits on the couch, tucking her feet underneath her, both hands gripping the coffee mug as she blows across the hot coffee.

"But my mom loved it. She's a lot like me. When my parents first moved up, Mom and I spent the whole first month being quintessential tourists. We must have gone to Paul Revere's house three times. We went on this whole Revolutionary spree. I re-read *Common Sense* and *The Federalist Papers* and Mom dragged me to the cemetery to see Samuel Adams' tombstone." She laughs, the sound musical.

I like seeing her like this. Comfortable and at ease, surrounded by her books and holding her coffee mug. Something in my chest stirs. Memories from summers ago and moments from this past year, mixing together to fill me with a strange sense of nostalgia. But for what?

She takes a sip of her coffee and grins at me. "Did you and Easton do all the touristy things when you first moved here?"

It's an innocent question. A normal one. Suddenly, it bothers me that I never appreciated the enormously important piece of history I live in. I bite my lip and shake my head. "I'm embarrassed to say that I haven't."

Her mouth falls open. "You've never been to Paul Revere's house, have you?"

I shake my head again.

"Oh my God!" she declares, looking truly aghast. "Don't worry. I'll take you. I'm going to give you the best tour of Boston you've ever had."

"Shouldn't it be the other way around? You haven't even been here a year," I point out.

"True." She nods. "I'll take you around all the historical sites and—"

"I'll introduce you to the modern city."

"What does that entail?" She wrinkles her nose, skeptical.

"Restaurants, clubs, shopping. Have you dined at The Ivy yet? Or had margaritas at Jolene's? They have a great happy hour."

She shakes her head.

"Then you're missing out too, Little Indy. We'll each pick a day. One day, we do your Boston and one day, we do mine."

She grins, nodding. "Okay, I like this plan."

I take a sip of my coffee and smile back. "Not as much as me."

Indy rolls her eyes but her cheeks pink and she looks adorable. I don't remember the last time I enjoyed flirting so much but with Indy, it's effortless. She blushes easily but is playful and engaging and doesn't just agree with everything I say because of my public persona.

"When do you want to do this?" she asks.

I pause, thinking over my training schedule. "We have our season opener next week."

"I know."

"Are you coming to the game?"

"Of course."

"Really?" I ask, surprised.

She gives me a strange look. "Yes, my cousin is the captain."

"Oh yeah." I laugh, feeling like an idiot. Of course her entire family will show up to support Austin. The Merricks are nothing if not a tight family unit. "Well, training before the game is pretty intense but we will definitely have Sunday off."

"Are you sure you want to spend it with me? It's your only day off."

I shrug. "I'm sure it will be better than playing Xbox."

She wrinkles her nose but then her expression smooths out and her eyes glitter. "You may be singing a different tune once you're sitting on a Duck Tour."

I grimace, recalling the strange-looking tanks that turn into boats for tours around the city. If East could see me in this moment, he'd junk punch me and ask where the hell my manhood went. These are the types of things you do for your girl. Not for the girl you're desperately craving but never going to make yours. "We're going all in?"

"All in, Scotch," she taunts, her gaze meeting mine over the rim of her coffee mug.

I'd be lying if I said the challenge in it didn't entice me.

11

INDY

"You were serious about the Duck Tour?" he accuses as I hold up two tickets for Boston's famous Duck Tour and fan myself with them.

"You're going to thank me later when we drink a pint at Cheers and chuckle over our favorite memories from this must-do city attraction."

Noah tosses his head back and laughs. He's glorious when he does that. Like a Roman emperor meets a modern-day Casanova meets a supreme athlete. *Okay, rein it in, Indiana.*

"Come on. Pretend, for one day, that you're visiting Boston for the first time. Try and see it as an outsider would. It really is beautiful and brimming with so much history, so much character and charm, just," I sigh, more dreamily than I intend, "life."

Noah snickers but agrees to take it all in stride. Even though it's early October and a winter chill hangs in the air, it isn't unbearable. In fact, the lineup for my favorite city tour is intense. In front of us, a family of six waits with kids jumping up and down and spilling popcorn along the curb. Noah smiles at one of the little girls. She sticks her tongue out at him and I crack up. "First female immune to your charms," I joke.

"My demographic is considerably older," he agrees.

The massive tank pulls up to the side of the curb and people begin singling on, pausing for the obligatory tourist photo.

"Yay!" I point, gripping his forearm with both of mine. I usher Noah to the front. He wraps an arm around my shoulders and I try not to lean too much into him, which is tough since it's pretty much the number one thing I want to do. That and have sex with him again, which is so not happening.

"Smile," the photographer orders. I cheese hard.

Once we climb up onto the tank, the breeze kicks up and I shiver, tucking my hands into my scarf.

"You warm enough?" Noah asks, placing an arm around my shoulders and pulling me closer.

Now I am. Thank God those words don't fall from my desperate-for-his-touch mouth. Instead, I look up and nod, trying my best not to make star beams at him with my eyes.

Noah Scotch is off-limits. He's a hockey player. A man who wants none of the same things as me. A guy whose career and ambitions will always come before mine.

If I constantly remind myself of these important facts, I may be able to get through this day date without throwing myself at him. Maybe.

"All right, ladies, gentlemen, and families of all sizes. We're about to get this party started. Welcome to the Duck Tour!" the guide calls out into his microphone and everyone claps and cheers. We roll through downtown Boston with our guide pointing out historical landmarks and explaining their backstories.

Noah leans toward me and whispers, "Your mouth is hanging open."

I snap it closed and turn to look at him.

He's grinning. "I thought you've been on this tour before."

"This is my third one."

He snickers. "Okay, you are a nerd."

I smile back, nodding in agreement.

"But a hot nerd." He bites his bottom lip.

"Teacher's pet." I pat his hand. Surprise zips through me as he clasps my fingers in his and holds on to them for a beat too long.

"I bet all the guys in your class have the hots for you," he says, his tone more serious than a moment ago.

"The guys in my class are barely legal."

"Doesn't mean they're not crushing on you."

I shrug. "It's more the TA's than the students in my classes."

His brow furrows. "TA's?"

"Teaching assistants. They're usually grad school students who pick up the TA gig as a work-study or a way to reduce their tuition costs."

"And you have one?"

"Two actually."

"And he hits on you?" Noah's lips press together and I can't tell if he's simply curious or a little jealous.

Is it pathetic that I want him to be a tiny bit jealous?

I grin coyly and lift an eyebrow. "I wouldn't call it *hitting* on me. He's just flirtatious, is all."

"Flirtatious," Noah repeats, an undercurrent to his tone.

"You're going to miss the best part," I sidetrack him as the tank eases into the Charles River and turns into a boat. "Ta-da!" I throw my arms open wide.

Noah smiles and wraps an arm casually around my shoulders. I face forward, listening to the tour guide. But I don't miss the way Noah studies my profile for a long moment. Or that he doesn't remove his arm from around my shoulder. Or that he looks at me with more heat than *just* a friend.

After our boat tour, I take Noah to Cheers for lunch.

"It's a classic," I explain as I order two pints for us.

"You know, I can't believe I've been living in this city for as long as I have and I've never been here." He looks around the old bar and pub appreciatively.

"You must have missed the long weekends Aunt Mary came to town to visit Austin before she and Uncle Joe moved here."

"I begged off them," he admits, chuckling. "She used to take Austin and the girls on intense history tours."

"I know. I used to beg on them. I think I can credit Aunt Mary for my love of history."

Noah glances at me, his expression curious. "What was your childhood like?"

I pick up my spoon to dig into my New England clam chowder but pause at his tone. "What do you mean?"

He shrugs sheepishly and shakes his head. "Never mind."

"No, ask me."

"I just, I wonder what it was like growing up as an only child. I mean, your dad was on the road a lot and you mostly saw your cousins in the summer…"

"It was okay," I say slowly, thinking back to the long stretches of time when it was just me and mom. We were always close, always able to make any of Dad's career changes work, fit seamlessly into our lives. But that was more her doing, her enthusiasm, than mine. "As far as childhoods go, mine was pretty wonderful. I mean, my mom is *that* mom. The one who volunteers as class mom and bakes homemade brownies for my ballet fundraising initiatives. It was lonely in the sense that I never had the great chaos that Claire grew up in. I didn't have a ton of friends and our house was never full, although it definitely seemed that way when Dad was home." I smile, recalling my Dad's infectious energy. "I had a few close friends who had brothers and sisters. My best friend in Tampa, Aid, was always around, just down the street. My friend Rosa is one of six."

Noah whistles, popping a French fry into his mouth.

"Sleepovers at her house were the best. Her older brothers always had friends around and they would let us stay up and drink beer or wine coolers with them." I laugh, my mind conjuring up a handful of memories I forgot about. "Rosa and I were so straight-laced, such good students, focused, you know?" I glance at Noah and he's staring at me like I'm telling some riveting tale instead of a bunch of random memories from high school. "Anyway, those nights were me stepping out of my comfort zone and they were fun. But I missed my dad. Mom missed him too." I shrug. "It's just, it's not a life I want going forward. The nights on the road, the early mornings sitting in ice rinks, the sacrifices you have to make year after year, season after season… My mom put her whole life on hold every time Dad asked her to. And we were lucky because we stayed in Tampa for nine years. For most families, there's even more uncertainty, more moves, just more giving of themselves and giving up their dreams…" I trail off, biting my lip and shooting Noah an apologetic look. "Sorry. I didn't mean—"

"No," he cuts me off. "You're being honest."

I take a mouthful of soup and moan. "Here." I hold my spoon out to him. "Try this. It's tradition."

"Tradition?"

"Mom's and mine."

He grumbles but I can tell he likes being in on it. He takes my spoon and dips it into the bowl, taking a mouthful. "This is so good," he manages to say around the chowder.

"See? I won't steer you wrong, Scotch."

He smiles at me.

"What was your childhood like?" I ask after a beat.

He shrugs and his features shift, a shutter coming down over his eyes. "It was okay."

"Okay…"

"Wasn't like yours. My mom wasn't *that* mom. My dad was an alcoholic. Our house wasn't the kind of house I would invite friends over to. For the most part, it was just me and East until we met Austin and started spending loads of time, weeks in the summer really, at Mary and Joe's."

I nod, remembering how the Scotch brothers were always around.

"It's lucky you and East had each other."

"Yeah, East and hockey are the only two constants in my life," he admits, picking up his pint and taking a long pull. "And now, only hockey really. It's the only thing I feel like I can commit myself to and not be disappointed. We're going all the way this season; I won't settle for anything less. Besides, when East gets out of rehab, he'll be coming home. I need to make sure he has something to look forward to, something to work toward. I won't let him down again."

I bite my lower lip, understanding all the words he's not saying. Like how hockey is his lifeline. How he's scared for his brother and for the team. How he feels like things are spiraling out of his control and if he can just manage his performance on the ice, if he can just play his best, he'll still have hockey. "I get it," I say softly.

"Do you?" he asks, his face severe but his tone quiet.

I nod. "I do. Hockey has never let you down."

"No," he agrees. "Not yet at least."

I pick up my pint glass and hold it up to him. "To your best season yet."

His eyes sweep over my face as he clinks his glass against mine. "Cheers at Cheers, Indy."

I snort. "Who's being a nerd now?"

Noah laughs and takes a swig of his beer.

Our conversation transitions to lighter topics and I find myself enjoying his company, excited to learn more about him, happy to just be in this moment, without worrying what comes next.

12

NOAH

"Thank you for today, Little Indy," I say as we stop in front of my brownstone.

"Anytime, Noah. Thanks for being a good sport."

I chuckle, tipping my head to the front door. My hands are stuffed in my pockets as the breeze picks up, and as much as I want to stay and chat with Indy, I don't want us to freeze while we do it. "Want to come in?"

She hesitates and a ripple of dejection swims in my stomach, which is ridiculous because we just spent the entire day together.

Before I can tell her not to sweat it she dips her head and says, "Okay."

"I've got coffee," I joke, knowing caffeine is her weakness.

She laughs and follows me into my house, tossing her purse down on the kitchen island. "I'll never say no to a coffee."

"I'll remember that." I pop a pod into the Nespresso machine and turn, bracing my elbows on the kitchen island.

Indy slides onto a barstool and grins at me. "I had fun today."

"Me too," I agree. "Being with you is…easy. Not complicated."

"That's a good thing, right?"

"Yeah." I wonder why she would think it isn't a good thing.

She shrugs. "You looked annoyed when you said it."

I shake my head even though she's probably right. It's strange to me, how I can hang with a woman and have it be so natural. Without the usual expectations and pressures that hang around me like a noose with most of my interactions with women. Even with Courtney, I felt like I was walking on eggshells sometimes. "Milk or cream?" I ask, picking up her coffee mug.

"Cream please."

I fix her coffee and place it down in front of her.

"You excited for the season opener?" She takes a sip of coffee and groans appreciatively. I feel that groan everywhere. Her eyes flutter closed and a small, satisfied smile crosses her mouth and my hands clench into fists.

Things may be easy with Indy Merrick but they can't be this casual.

My hands yearn to reach out and glide over her smooth skin. My mouth waters at the thought of getting another taste of her. Jesus, how is she this tempting sitting in my kitchen on a Sunday drinking coffee? Why can't I shake my hunger for her?

"Noah?" she asks, peering at me in concern.

I clear my throat. What the fuck were we talking about? The game. "Yeah, yeah, I'm excited for it."

Her eyebrows dip down over her nose. "You okay?"

I sigh, raking a hand over my head. Do I tell her? Just lay

it all out? Why the fuck not? I've never been known to mince words before. "I lied to you."

She rears back like I startled her and I curse myself for being such an idiot. "About what?"

"I don't want to be *just* friends, Indiana. I may be crazy presumptuous right now but the other night..." I trail off, gauging her reaction.

"The other night what?" she whispers, her eyes searching mine.

"The other night was better than great. It was, fuck, I can't stop thinking about it. About you, in my bed, and I want you there again."

Indy stares at me in shock for a full second and I want to throat punch myself just to distract my thoughts from the wary expression crossing her face. Did I mess everything up? Indy clears her throat and says the most beautiful words I've ever heard, "I felt it too."

"You did?" I reach forward and tuck some of her hair behind her ear, my hand cupping her face. God, her skin is so smooth. So soft.

She nods.

"I don't want to be *just* friends, Indy."

"You said that already."

I smile. "I know. But I don't want to lead you on either."

"You're not. I get what you're saying. Today was fun, it was easy and chill. But if we hang out and have some fun and things happen..."

"If things happen..." I repeat, desperate for her to finish that thought. Does she want things to happen? Does she want to do this, things, with me, knowing it won't lead to anything real?

"If things happen and we both know the score, then what's the harm in that?" she asks finally and excitement bursts in my veins like Pop Rocks. She wants this, me, as much as I'm craving her.

I lean over the island and turn her face so she's staring right at me. I need her to understand my next words and be okay with them before I drag her to me and kiss her senseless. "No harm, babe. Just promise me, you'll be straight with me if things get too…complicated."

"Same goes for you," she says simply and I can tell she means it. Jesus, who is this woman? I've yet to meet a woman so sure of a casual, fun, hook-up with me and yet, Indy has surprised me at every turn.

I place a hand over my heart and don't miss the way her eyes zero in on the movement, how the tip of her tongue peeks out between her lips. "Same goes for me," I promise.

"Cool." Indy grins. When she looks at me, I don't see indecision or uncertainty in her eyes. I see a woman who truly understands the score and wants the same thing that I want: some fun, some genuine conversation, and some smoking hot sex.

"Would now be too early to get naked?" I ask, keeping my voice light in case I have to turn my question into a joke. But I'm not fucking joking.

Indy places down her coffee mug and stands. In one stroke, she tugs her sweater off and stands before me, all creamy skin and delicious curves, clad in a black lace bra. "Not too early."

I growl, walking toward her. She grins, backing away toward the stairs. Before we begin to climb them to my bedroom she pauses and glances at me over her shoulder. "I should tell you, Noah, that I don't usually do this type of thing."

"What type of thing?" I ask even though I know the answer.

"Casual."

Some of my excitement evaporates. Is this going to be too difficult for her to commit to? The fact that there is no commitment. "Okay…"

"But with you"—she shakes her head, her eyes gleaming —"I don't know. It's almost a relief that we have a history, a friendship, so that I can be myself with you and know that you're not taking it the wrong way."

Relief washes through me at her words. "Just be straight with me, Indy."

She blushes, swiping her tongue along her bottom lip. When she meets my gaze again, the heat in hers is undeniable. Her nipples harden, tempting me through the lacy cups of her bra. Jesus, I want her in my bed. Now. Five minutes ago.

"I want you, Noah Scotch. I want you to set my body on fire and make me feel all the things I've been missing out on."

At the truth in her words, at the plea in her tone, I growl and swoop her into my arms. Carrying her up the stairs, I love the sound of her breathless giggle. I love the feel of her silky hair sliding across my arms.

"I got you, Indy." I toss her in the center of my bed.

She smirks at me as I yank my shirt off and pop the button on my jeans. I stride toward her and wrap my hands around her ankles, tugging until she's spread out beneath me. I peel off her leggings and groan at the sight of her black silk thong that leaves so very little to the imagination. "You always wear underwear like this?"

"I like the way they look." She offers a non-answer that intrigues me as much as it irritates me. Do other guys see her like this? No, she told me she doesn't do casual. Still…the thought of her with another guy bothers me even though it shouldn't. Even though I don't want it to.

But I let that flicker of annoyance take hold as I crawl up Indy's body and fuse my mouth with hers. I let my irritation of thinking about her with other men fuel my actions as I claim her in the middle of a Sunday afternoon in the center of my bed until we're both breathless. Until our bodies hum with adrenaline and quake with need.

Until I slide inside of her and swear. She moans loudly, her fingernails digging into my forearms as I bring her to the peak of a mountain and jump off the damn cliff after her.

As we come down from our mutual bliss, I stare into Indiana's eyes and almost fucking drown.

Not that I'd tell her that. Not that I'd even admit it to myself.

And that, is my first major mistake where Indiana Merrick is concerned.

13

INDY

"Are you like, his sex slave?" Claire whispers way too loudly for Sunday night's family dinner.

I kick her under the table and she winces.

Two seats over, Austin turns toward us and we both drop our heads.

"Sorry," Claire whispers again. "I'm just so curious. And desperate for information because I haven't gotten laid in way too long."

"Claire," I hiss.

She shrugs unapologetically. "After the way he stared at you at Taps after the Hawks won their season opener, you can't blame me for asking. All the WAGs are wondering about you two, you know."

"Seriously?" I wrinkle my nose, hating the thought that Noah and I and our mutual, non-committed, fun fling is feeding gossip fodder.

"You can hardly blame them, Indy." Claire turns toward me. "One, Scotch didn't let you out of his sight the entire evening. Two, he hasn't been that way with anyone since Courtney."

"This is nothing like him and Courtney," I say, wanting to clarify that Noah and I aren't serious. At all.

"Duh." My cousin snorts. "You're a million times better than Courtney."

"That's not what I meant," I point out but Claire shrugs.

"What are you girls giggling about?" Uncle Joe asks from the head of the table. Claire quickly scoops half a chicken thigh into her mouth so all eyes turn toward me.

I kick Claire again under the table and she coughs around her full mouth.

"Nothing," I say to the skeptical looks of our parents and Austin. "Just that Claire is on the job and apartment hunt."

"Really, love?" Aunt Mary asks, her eyes zeroing in on her daughter. "You know there's no rush, right? You can stay here as long as you like."

This time, the toe of Claire's boot finds my shin and I wince at the weight she put behind it.

"Thanks, Mom," Claire says lightly. "Indy and I were just discussing options, that's all. Rielle might have a friend looking for a roommate too."

"How is Rielle? She hasn't been here in ages," Aunt Mary remarks.

Claire huffs. "I know. She works all the time. Indy and I are going to grab coffee with her and catch up this week."

"Well, you know we'd miss having you here if this thing with Rielle's friend works out," Uncle Joe adds, laying on another layer of guilt.

Austin snorts under his breath and I drop my head to keep from laughing out loud.

It's no secret that Claire is desperate to move out of my aunt and uncle's home. Mostly because they still treat her like a little kid and Claire has a big personality. The kind of personality that doesn't want to be reined in by anyone, especially not her dad.

"I know." She grins at her dad and shoots mine a pleading look for help.

Dad covers up his laughter by coughing into his hand, and changes the subject. "Looks like Mike is off to a great season."

"Oh, he's playing so much more now that he's in New York," Aunt Mary agrees, clasping her hands together. "I thought it was going to be such a tough transition but Vanny loves the city and the two of them are happy there. I really hope they have a baby soon."

"Mary," Uncle Joe cautions.

"What?" she asks him, gesturing to the table. "I'm just confiding in family."

"Here we go," Austin mutters. As the parents launch into a conversation about grandkids, Austin looks at Claire and me. "You girls are staying out of trouble?"

"Of course," Claire huffs.

"Me?" I point to myself. "When have I ever gotten into trouble?"

"When you spend too much time with this one." Austin points at his sister, speaking the truth from years of experience.

I shrug, stuffing a large forkful of pasta into my mouth.

"Hey, how's East doing?" Claire asks Austin.

He sighs, rubbing a hand across his forehand. "He's doing pretty good. Really focused on his recovery. I know it's good, obviously as the team captain, it's great, that Sims is playing so well. I'm just worried East isn't going to have a position to come back to by the time all is said and done."

Claire's face falls. "Have you seen him again?"

"Yeah, two days ago. Noah's visiting him now."

My ears perk up at this. Noah didn't mention visiting his brother. I wonder if it's hard for him, to see Easton struggling the way he is. I wonder if he's talking about it with anyone since he hasn't said anything to me.

Pulling my phone out of my pocket, I check to see that my family members are all engaged in conversation before I fire off a text.

Me: Hey! Busy tonight?

It only takes a few moments for him to respond, which makes me smile.

Noah: Busy doing you?

I snort.

Me: What happened to not being a booty call?

Noah: You're a 100 times more than that and you know it.

Me: How's East?

Bubbles appear and disappear at the bottom of the screen several times before it stays blank. I frown.

"Indy?" Mom's voice cuts through my thoughts.

I glance up.

Everyone is staring at me and I flush under their looks.

"Yes?" I ask, wondering what I missed.

"How's everything going with the trip you're planning?" Mom asks.

"Oh!" I smile in relief. "It's going great. I chose the final eight students and two backups for the travel and we've launched into some methods for gathering information in the field. It's…" I fill them in on the logistics surrounding the trip. By the time I'm finished, everyone seems satisfied with my response and new clusters of conversation break out.

I peek at my phone screen again.

Noah: He's okay.

Noah: Where are you?

I frown at his message, not understanding why he's asking.

Me: Aunt Mary's

Noah: Oh. Cool. See you after?

Me: I've got to stop at campus. I'll come by around nine?

Noah. Okay. See you then.

Me: See you

I slip my phone back in my pocket. Next to me, Claire gives me a knowing look and I smile but inside, something feels off. Unsettled. It's unlike Noah to be so abrupt, even in a text message.

Gah, what is wrong with me?

I promised myself I wouldn't read too much into everything, not this time. Definitely not with Noah Scotch.

Taking a deep breath, I pick up my wine glass and take a long sip.

After the busy week I had, a night in Noah's bed will do me good, even if his conversation leaves me wanting more.

HE'S QUIETER THAN NORMAL, a little lost in his head.

"You okay?" I ask, dropping onto his couch and stacking my feet on the ottoman.

"Yeah," Noah sighs, glancing at me. "Saw East today." He shakes his head. "It just sucks, seeing him there, knowing how hard he's working at things. And here I am." He waves his beer bottle in the air.

I offer him a sympathetic shrug. "You didn't do anything wrong by being able to have a beer."

"No," Noah agrees, tipping the bottle back and draining its contents. His eyes pierce mine. "But neither did Easton."

"I'm sorry, Noah. Do you want to talk about it?" I keep my tone neutral but lean forward, hoping he confides in me.

He watches me for a long beat. When he blinks, some of the aloofness in his gaze fades, desire filling its place. "I know a better way to work out my mood."

I snort. "Cute."

"Get over here, Little Indy," he beckons.

Standing, I walk over to him slowly. Noah bites his bottom lip, his eyes scanning my body. When I'm within arm's length, he reaches out and tugs me forward by my belt loops. "I'm happy you're here."

It's sweet and my heart rate ticks up at the sincerity in his tone. I slip onto his lap, straddling him. My hands rest on top of his shoulders. Noah's hand cups my cheek affectionately, his thumb brushing over my cheekbone. "Me too," I murmur before I dip my head and kiss his lips.

He pulls me closer, kissing me softly and slowly. I savor the taste of his kiss before his tongue slips into my mouth, dancing with mine. Noah's hands fall to my hips, squeezing and kneading as I drop even lower on his lap. Slanting my head, I deepen our connection and let out a mewl as I feel him harden beneath me. I grind against him, the friction of my jeans against his length causing desire to pool between my legs.

"Jesus," Noah breathes, ripping his mouth from mine and kissing the underside of my jaw. His hand slips underneath my shirt and works it up, until it's bunched over my bra and my breasts are in his line of vision. He wastes no time.

"Noah," I breathe out, cupping the back of his head as he yanks the cup of my bra down and fastens his mouth around my nipple. My eyes close as sensations rock through me. Noah's mouth is hot on my skin, his one hand buried in my hair, his other teasing between my thighs. I groan, knowing I should be embarrassed, but too far past caring.

I'm nearly twenty-eight years old and here I am, writhing against this man, still fully clothed, and too goddamn desperate for his touch to rein it in. Noah's mouth streaks across my chest as he latches onto my other breast. I'm grinding against him as hard as I can, swearing at the denim prohibiting our contact.

Noah bites down gently and I cry out before he flips me onto the couch. My back hits the cushions and he hovers over me, his eyes wild. "Need you, Indy." He grabs at his shirt behind his neck and tugs it off. It falls to the floor and for a second, I wonder how he always manages to do that so gracefully. But then he's popping the button on my jeans and I'm pulling my shirt over my head.

In a matter of minutes, we're naked and panting, staring at each other like we can't believe how quickly we got to this point. My eyes zero in on his hard cock and I lick my lips, reaching out to wrap my hand around the base. Noah swears, his eyes dropping to half-mast. I stroke him gently, liking the silky feel of him against my palm. His eyes devour my body like a feast, his fingers caressing my skin.

"Give me a minute, babe." Noah brushes a kiss across my mouth. "Need to run and grab a condom."

The thought of him leaving in this moment, even for an instant, fills me with impatience. Need pools in my core, my body so freaking tight, I could snap. Still, I nod. Because there's no way to ruin casual faster than not using a condom. Noah swears and slides off of me, taking the stairs two at a time. I giggle as I watch his naked ass disappear and reappear three seconds later, a box of condoms in hand.

"Feeling pretty confident?" I tease.

Noah chuckles, grabbing a foil packet from the box and

dropping it next to the couch. "Don't know what it is about you, Indy, but I bet we could burn through the entire box." He sheaths himself and shoots me a playful look. "It'd be all you though."

"Obviously." I grin.

Noah resettles over me and gives me one long look that I can't decipher. Then, his mouth finds mine again and my laughter turns into a whimper. A needy, desperate whimper. I reach for him again, picking up where we left off.

His eyes close, his cock twitching under my touch. His abdomen tightens, his shoulders roll, and I tug him closer, desperate to feel his weight over me, taste his skin, get lost in his touch. He forces his eyes open and they pierce mine.

I hook my leg behind his knee until he falls forward, careful to brace his weight without crushing my body. "Fuck," he murmurs, kissing me hard.

In an instant, everything shifts. The slow and playful morphs into desperate and hot. The soft rages into hard. I feel Noah's hands everywhere, his mouth pouring need into mine.

"Look at me, Indy," he demands, his tone ragged.

I force my eyes open and take in his expression. His mouth is parted, his breathing labored. His eyes are black, more intense than I've ever seen them. He doesn't blink as he presses into me and I cry out, arching into him.

Noah gathers me to his chest and stills for one beat before pulling back. He works a rhythm that has me seeing stars, my body burning hot and cold. His fingertips dragging against my skin feels like a live wire and his breath in my ear causes goosebumps to spread over my skin.

"Noah," I urge him to move faster, moving my hips up to meet his.

He swears and quickens his pace. My body coils tighter and tighter, my core pulsing, my fingers clutching his back.

Then, I break, screaming out his name and shattering into a million beads of bliss.

Noah follows immediately afterwards and collapses on top of me before rolling so we're both on our sides, my ass hovering over the edge of the couch.

"That was intense," I breathe out, my heart galloping.

Noah's fingers dip into my waist as he growls, "What the hell am I doing with you, Indy? What the hell was that?"

I snort, keeping my eyes closed and enjoying this moment a hell of a lot more than I should. Considering it's casual. Considering it's fun, sexy times.

But damn does my heart sing at Noah's words.

14

NOAH

I flip the puck to Sims, noting from my peripheral vision that Austin blocks for him. Sims breaks away, perfectly executing a wrist shot as the buzzer for the second period sounds. The team celebrates, smacking Sims' helmet and back. As we collapse onto the bench, guzzling water, an energy shift seems to wash over the bench.

For the first time since Sims claimed my brother's spot four weeks ago, the team embraces him. Words are exchanged but the edge is gone, playful punches don't hold the same strength, the veil of distrust has been lifted.

Sims catches my eye and dips his chin. I lift mine slightly and we come to an understanding. He's my teammate and I'm going to do everything I can to push the team forward. But I'll always have my brother's back.

The realization settles me some and feels good, as if I've come to an important decision after long nights of it weighing on my mind, zapping my energy.

"Listen up," Coach Phillips walks down the bench, rattling off instructions and tweaking some of our play. We're up 3–1 against the Seattle Serpents and we need this win, need to keep the start of our season successful with the right morale to carry us forward. "Don't lose your edge. You've got one period left," Coach bellows, slapping our helmets as he passes.

When the buzzer sounds again and we line up for the face-off, Austin tosses me a grateful grin and I know we're doing the right thing. We're backing Sims to ensure he becomes part of the team, we're creating a rhythm with him that may be more promising than our natural ease with Easton. We're doing what's right for the team, even if it isn't what's best for my brother. But then again, I think back to everything I've learned from Indy, maybe it is. Maybe what's best for Easton aren't the assumptions I've been carrying around for ages. Maybe it isn't even hockey.

The puck is dropped and play begins. Tuning out the noise in my head, I focus in on the puck. Austin passes to me and I skate furiously up the side of the rink, flipping a backhand pass to Sims before I'm body checked into the boards. We play hard for the next four minutes until a fight breaks out between Torsten and a Serpent. Within moments, the entire team on the ice is involved and the whistles are blowing angrily from the referees with both coaches shouting at their players. Once the fight is broken up, I spot Austin's grin. Sims jumped in first for Torsten and there's no better way to cement team unity than by taking a punch intended for another guy. Torsten's lip is bleeding but the Seattle winger looks worse off.

I chuckle, scratching my cheek. God, I've missed this game. I've missed this rush. I've missed it all since the end of last season. I glance up to the box where the WAGs always sit. When I spot Indy's face, I smile.

Seeing her here, cheering us on, fills me with even more

excitement for tonight. Adrenaline buzzes in my veins and I lose myself once more to the game I love.

After we secure our fourth win this season, Boston celebrates. Good energy and vibes dance over the team and we all agree to head to Taps, one of our team favorites and frequently visited bars.

I shower quickly in the locker room, dressing in dark jeans and a black sweater. My cheek is red from where I got slammed but other than that, I clean up pretty well.

"Want to ride together?" Austin asks as I close my locker.

"Isn't your family here?"

"Yeah. We're grabbing a bite before I meet the team for drinks. Come with us," he offers, the way he always does.

In the past, East and I would rarely join his family after games, knowing it was a nice opportunity for him to catch up with his parents and sisters. Plus, it was understood that East and I would grab a bite together too. But now, with Indy's family living in Boston and East gone, the dinners have become less core family and it makes it easier for me to shrug and say, "Yeah, sure."

"Let's go." Austin starts for the door, smacking Torsten on the back.

Torst glances up, his phone glued to his ear, his expression tight.

"See you at Taps?" Austin asks.

Torsten nods and shoots us a half grin but I can tell he's stressed about something. I clasp his arm as I pass and his grin turns real.

"Hey Ryan, you coming?" Austin calls out to James.

James looks up and offers us a tight smile but shakes his head. "I have to get home."

"Good game, man," I say as I pass him. If I thought this year was hard for me, it's been pure hell for James.

"I saw Indy sitting with the WAGs," I say as we leave the arena. I liked seeing her up there more than I should. Because she wasn't up there as my girl and for a second, a part of me wished she was.

Austin chuckles. "I bet Claire dragged her along. She's on a mission to get Indy out in the world."

"What do you mean?"

He glances at me over the hood of his car as he pulls open the driver's side door. "The WAGs talk about real things happening in their lives."

"Girl talk?" I ask skeptically, opening the passenger door.

Austin ducks and slides into the car and I follow. He flips the ignition.

"They talk about trips they're planning and the best primary schools to enroll their kids. They talk about house hunting in Boston and sales that are happening at different boutiques. They talk about their own businesses and managing a business while moving..." He shrugs. "They talk about a lot of things that don't involve being completely absorbed in some textbook espousing political theories. Moving here was the best thing my cousin did since going away to university after that asshat broke her heart. It finally got her to pull her nose from a book and stop studying all the time and enjoy life as it's happening around her."

The asshat that broke her heart. Jace Edwards.

"What was the deal with her and Jace anyway?" I ask, keeping my voice casual as I pull on my seatbelt.

"He played her the way he plays all the women in his life," Austin answers, pulling out of the arena's parking lot and pointing the car toward the restaurant. "I hate talking about a player's personal life but Jace fucked with Indy's head for a long time. Always tried to make her feel that his life, his priorities, hockey, and his career were so much more important than hers. I hated how he talked down to her, like what she was going to school for was stupid since she was going to end up with him and just follow him around from city to city so he could play hockey. Drove my uncle fucking nuts."

I swallow past the angry lump forming in my throat. What a dick. I could see him doing it though. Jace Edwards has always been an entitled, arrogant, man-child. He acts like he's God's gift to hockey (he's not), women (he's definitely not), and life in general (what a joke).

"Didn't she just kick him to the curb?" I ask.

Austin shakes his head, stopping at a red light. "I mean, eventually. But not until he really stripped down her self-esteem, made her question herself and her future, and then fucking cheated on her with another player's fiancée."

My hand tightens into a fist on my thigh. I fucking hate that Jace, that a guy like Jace, would cause Indy to question herself. I really hate that he cheated on her. And I absolutely abhor that it was with another player's fiancée. That one hits too damn close to home.

Damn. What a piece of work.

"But she's doing good here, in Boston?" I ask.

Austin narrows his eyes and swings his gaze toward mine. "What's with all the questions?"

"Nothing, just curious."

"About Indy?"

"Yeah, man. She's an awesome girl."

"She's my cousin."

"That doesn't make her any less awesome."

Austin snickers, shaking his head. "She doesn't date hockey players."

I bite the corner of my mouth to keep from saying anything.

Austin's laughter increases. "I'm serious, man. She has sworn off hockey players, much to my uncle's delight."

"I just like seeing her, that's all. She's like a breath of fresh air after a shitty year," I finally say, not wanting to admit just how much real estate Little Indy Merrick is taking up in my mind. And not wanting to dismiss the fact that I'm into her either. Jesus, what a limbo to be in.

Austin pulls into a parking spot and turns off the car. He stares at me for a long beat. "Indy's special, Scotch. She's not like the girls you're used to."

I scowl. "What do you mean the girls I'm used to?"

"She's not like Courtney."

"No shit."

Austin shrugs. "I'm just saying, she's special."

"I know that. That's why I like her."

"And she doesn't date hockey players."

"You already said that."

He lifts an eyebrow, his intent clear. I'm not going to end up with his cousin. "I'm saying it again."

I shake my head, forcing a smile. "I heard you the first time, Merrick."

He opens the car door. "Just making sure, Scotch."

I follow Austin into the restaurant. As soon as we cross the threshold, fans are cheering and clapping. We're ushered quickly to the table as a few people even stand from their chairs to applaud our performance tonight. Austin and I grin and wave and say a lot of "thank you's."

When we arrive at the table in the back of the restaurant, Austin cringes and I crack up at the balloons tied to the back of his chair. I swear, Mary Merrick is my favorite human on Earth. It doesn't matter that her son is captain of an NHL team, he's still her little boy and she still does things like buy balloons for his chair and send cupcakes to the team locker room on his birthday.

My laughter dies as she springs into action, untying some of Austin's balloons and adding them to the chair beside his. "For you, my dear." She points at me.

Austin snorts and I punch him in the shoulder.

"Great game, guys," Indy's dad says, ushering us to our chairs. I can tell he's holding back his laughter from Mary's antics.

Claire rushes us, giving us each a hug. Vanny kisses our cheeks and Mike shakes our hands. Indy wraps us in quick hugs, blushing when I smile at her.

We all sit down and appetizers arrive as if on demand while we take a few moments to scan the menu and choose entrees. Wine is poured, bread rolls are buttered, and the happy, loud chatter of the Merrick family fills my ears. Glancing around the table, a pang hits my chest. I wish Easton was here. But when I spot Indy's glowing face, her eyes shimmering at whatever tale Vanny and her husband Mike are recounting, some of my worries ease. Instead, I let Indy's sunshine and warmth wash over me and I realize just how happy I am that she's here.

15

INDY

"You're coming," Claire demands.

"I feel like this is a theme in our lives," I counter, trying to beg off of drinks with the team tonight. Not because I don't want to go, I do. But because I have a full teaching day tomorrow and I'd rather not do it hungover.

"You don't have to drink," Claire promises.

I raise an eyebrow.

"Vanny's even coming!" She tries again and my resolve begins to crack. I've barely seen Savannah since she moved to New York. With her husband's hockey schedule and her own job as a teacher, she hasn't been back to Boston in over a month.

"Please, Indy." Savannah grips my arm and gives me her puppy-dog eyes. "Mike and I never get to come out with you guys."

"Yeah, Indy. Please." Mike pouts and I snort.

Rolling my eyes, I agree. "Okay, I'll come. But I can only have one drink."

Claire coughs.

"Two, max," I amend.

Claire whoops and Savannah hugs me closer.

I turn to say goodbye to my parents and aunt and uncle and thank them for dinner.

Mom hugs me goodbye. "Have fun, Indiana. Really, these are the nights you should go out and enjoy. The whole city is alive tonight."

I pull back and grin at her. "Mom, you're supposed to encourage me to go home and prepare for my classes."

She scoffs, humor in the lines around her mouth. "Please, Indiana, you've been over prepared for the past decade. Have a little fun."

I press a kiss to her cheek. "If you say so, Mom."

Dad wraps me in a big hug and slips me a $100, which always makes me laugh. I try to give it back to him but he shakes his head, his eyes bright. "You're still not tenured," he reminds me.

I roll my eyes and wave goodbye. While Savannah corrals Claire into her car with Mike, I'm ushered into the back seat of Austin's ride.

"Are you sure you don't mind us tagging along?" I ask my cousin as he pulls out of the parking lot.

He meets my gaze in the rearview mirror. "Nah, not tonight. Tonight, there will be loads of the wives and girl-friends and friends. It's a celebration. I'm glad you're coming, Indy."

"Me too," Noah says, turning around to meet my eyes as he says the words. My cousin flips him a look but Noah ignores it. "What's your poison tonight?"

I hold up a finger. "I can only have one drink."

Austin and Noah crack up.

"I'm serious. I have classes all day tomorrow."

"Yeah and don't you think the majority of the kids in your

classes are going to be hungover?" Austin glances at me in the rearview mirror again.

I roll my eyes. "That's not a good reason for me to throw out the rule book."

Austin chuckles. "You need to get out more, Indy."

"I know," I agree. My family's support is sometimes more stressful than encouraging. As if they have unlimited faith in my decisions.

"Any new updates about your student trip?" Noah asks and I don't miss the glare Austin shoots him.

Leaning back in my seat, I tell them more about the trip to Dhaka. "We're even going to Grameen Bank. Muhammad Yunus started it in the 1970s and…"

"Wow," Austin says, impressed. "What's the purpose of the research aspect?"

"Ideally, to write a paper for publication. It will focus on the role of women in a patriarchal society and how women push the advancement of their families, and thereby society, forward when they have more control over the finances. It will be a great opportunity for my students to dabble in field research and also contribute to a publication. I'm really excited about it, obviously, and want it to all work out. To be honest, I'm a little nauseous just thinking about all the responsibility of things that could go wrong."

Austin chuckles but Noah's eyes are warm when they seek me out again. He looks at me with such intensity, such understanding, that for a second, it's as if he sees all the way to my soul. Past my insecurities and doubts and to the heart of why this is so important to me.

"You're going to rock it, Indy. You speak about your work with so much passion and enthusiasm, so much optimism, that your students are lucky to have you as a role model."

His words rock through me, heartfelt and sincere and so encouraging. "Thank you, Noah."

My cousin's eyes flick back to mine again and I don't miss the scowl on his face. But when I look at Noah, I see the truth in his expression. He means what he says and his belief in me, someone who isn't related to me and obligated to support my decisions, fills me with an extra layer of confidence. I don't think he even realizes how much he soothes my nerves but he does.

Suddenly, I'm glad I came out tonight.

———————

TAPS IS RAUCOUS.

The energy is pulsing, the crowds are swarming, and the drinks are flowing. When we arrive, fans cheer and stand on barstools, hollering out their congratulations and gratitude. Austin and Noah flank me, and while my cousin always looks out for me, it's Noah who places his hand in the small of my back and shadows my frame, as if worried for my safety.

Austin and Noah stop several times to sign autographs and I don't miss the shade thrown my way. Women wearing low-cut shirts and more makeup than Sephora carries look at me with expressions ranging from curiosity to outright hatred. A chill works through my veins at the venom in their eyes and I falter back a step, right into the muscled wall of Noah's chest.

His hand drops to my hip to steady me but after he hands back the hat he signed, it stays there, familiar. Once Austin resumes pushing through the crowd, Noah grasps my hand in his and pulls me along, not caring one bit about the attention that our hand-holding garners. In fact, he seems oblivious to all the evil looks of women wearing his number, the sly smiles of random guys, and the double takes of a few members of his team.

We enter the private room at the back that Claire told me the team takes over after every home game. Noah guides me up to the bar and pulls a credit card from his wallet, tapping it against the bar ledge and smirking down at me. "What are you having, Little Indy?"

I smile, remembering how much I hated when Austin, Noah, and Easton called me Little Indy back when I was sixteen and desperate to be taken seriously. Now, it flickers to life as a private joke between us, losing its sting and taking on a whole new definition of sweet. I tap my fingertips against the bar's ledge, debating.

"I got you," Noah says after reading the indecision on my face. He gestures to the bartender and a few minutes later, the guy springs into action.

"What did you order?"

"My favorite."

"Uh-oh."

"I swear, it's really good. And, it won't make you feel sluggish tomorrow."

I quirk an eyebrow, waiting for an explanation.

"It's tequila and sprite." His arm brushes against my shoulder as he leans down, lowering his voice. "But don't tell anyone. I pretend it's this fancy, secret drink I like."

I chuckle, nodding in agreement. The good news is I like tequila. The bad news is I could get drunk off of Noah's proximity alone.

Noah slides his card across the bar as the bartender places down two drinks. "Hey Pete. Can I start a tab?"

"You got it, Scotch. Good game tonight." Pete takes the card and walks down the bar to serve other players.

Noah nudges my drink closer to my hand and picks up his

glass. "To your trip, Indy. May your research and publication be wildly successful." His tone is playful, his expression serious. It's alluring, how invested he is in my work. Back when I applied to colleges, Jace used to grumble and roll his eyes, wondering why I even needed an education when I would be taking care of his house and children. I cringe just thinking of what an idiot I was to ever see anything charming about Jace Edwards.

I clink my glass against Noah's. "Congratulations on your big fat W. You were stellar tonight."

He clutches his chest, his glass hovering in the space between us. "Stellar? My God, Indiana, coming from you that's quite the compliment." I grin and his expression softens. "Thank you." He takes a sip of his drink and I follow suit.

The drink is smooth and refreshing, going down easier than it should.

Claire appears at my side and hip checks me. I hold my drink far over the bar as a little of its contents splash over the side and onto my hand.

"Oops, sorry," Claire says, flashing me a fake grimace.

Noah grabs some bar napkins and presses them to my wrist as Vanny, Mike, Austin, and Torsten join us at the bar.

"You're already drinking?" Savannah laughs, pointing at me. "So much for one drink."

I blush and Torsten cracks a grin, brushing a kiss across my cheek. "Good to see you, sweetheart."

Claire rolls her eyes. "Such a charmer, Big Daddy," she teases him since he's the oldest guy on the team.

Mike laughs as Noah narrows his eyes and Austin pulls his teammate back a few paces. Mike turns to the bartender and gestures to the group. "I'm drinking with the wrong team tonight. Keep 'em coming," he jokes, since he was traded from Boston to New York last year. While it was a hard hit, the move turned out to be better for his career. He now sees more playing time and has a bit of distance from so many overwhelming family members as he and Vanny navigate their first few years of marriage.

Savannah snorts and throws her arms around her husband. He kisses the tip of her nose and the fact that they're so in love, even while juggling their new move, life in a new city, and his hectic schedule is remarkable.

Austin orders a round of shots.

Noah dips his head toward me again. "You don't have to drink it."

I raise an eyebrow. "And get made fun of by this crowd?" I jerk my thumb over my shoulder to my judgey cousins.

"I'll take it for you if you're worried," he offers.

I turn to look over my shoulder as Claire argues with Austin over something. Torsten has pulled Panda into our little group. As the bartender lines up shot glasses, the swell of bodies pushes toward the bar, and I'm pressed closer into Noah's frame. His chest shadows my back and when I bump into him, he doesn't shuffle back but his fingers graze the side of my outer thigh, beckoning me closer.

Jesus, what am I doing?

This is Noah Scotch. He's one of Austin's best friends. He was engaged less than a year ago. I'm about to out myself in front of my family and his team. *He's a hockey player.*

Apparently, my body doesn't give a shit about any of the logic running through my mind. I press into him, his warmth and his strength, until he wraps a hand around my hip, his fingertips brushing below my belly button. I shiver and he dips his head again.

I turn to peer up at him and my lips graze the underside of his jaw. Jesus, he's so close. My body flushes hot and cold at his proximity and some of the noise of Taps falls away as Noah's smooth jawline and his intense eyes, focused solely on mine, block everything else out.

I clear my throat. "I'll take the shot."

He stares at me for a long moment, a heaviness passing between us. Whatever this is, it's more than just casual. It's more than it's supposed to be and we both know it. Because it shouldn't be anything at all.

"Just one." His gaze bores into mine.

I nod, the tip of my nose sliding against his chin.

He shifts his weight and tucks me into his frame, as if I belong there. As if we've done this dance a million times before and it's just muscle memory at this point. But my body is like a live wire. Every breath Noah takes, every stroke of his fingers, every rumble of his chest travels through me with the intensity of a category five hurricane. I feel plunged underwater and lifted into the sky and wrapped in fire and ice.

I feel a thrill of anticipation, a desperate expectation, that I've never experienced before.

Vanny shoots me a look. Claire bites back her laughter. Mike is oblivious. Austin glares at Noah's hand where it rests on my stomach. He opens his mouth, but before any words come out, Torsten places a shot glass in his hand and passes one to me, winking.

Torsten holds his glass in the air, turning to stare at the faces of our little huddle by the bar. "To this season!" he shouts.

Additional shouting and cheering rings out as we all raise our glasses and slam our shots.

I barely taste the alcohol.

All I can focus on is the way Noah's arms feel around me and I don't ever want them to drop.

16

NOAH

"What's going on with you and Indy?" Torsten asks me an hour later.

I've been nursing the same drink since we all took shots at the bar. Claire and Vanny pulled Indy to the bathroom with them and Torsten wasted no time cornering me. I don't like the glint in his eyes or his tone and I feel my limbs lock down, defensive-like.

"Why are you asking?" I flip my chin at him.

He sighs and runs a hand over the lower portion of his face. "Relax, Romeo. I'm not trying to move in on your girl."

"She's not—"

He waves a hand, silencing me. "The girl you've got your hands all over to warn everyone else back?"

I shrug because that's pretty correct. But I hate the thought of any of the guys here trying to ply Indy with drinks, especially when she's so concerned about her work and her commitment to her students. I hate the thought of any of them flirting with her or putting their hands on her even more.

In fact, since the moment I saw her at the game, the only

thing I can think about is having her again. Tonight. Now. It's irrational, it's dangerous, but it doesn't change a damn thing.

"Look, I'm only asking because Austin looks like he wants to deck you," Torsten says casually but I note the way his gaze slides down the bar to where Austin is talking with his brother-in-law. "So, whatever the deal is, you need to figure it out. Indy isn't just some puck bunny."

I rear back, offended he would even suggest something so ridiculous.

He sighs again and shakes his head. "Damn, Noah. Stop taking everything so personally. I'm looking out for you, man. My point is you need to either back off and stop acting like you're making a play for Indy's affections—" He grins, impressed with himself for delivering that message so delicately.

I flip him the middle finger.

Torsten laughs. "Or, you need to know what the hell you're doing about your attraction for her so when Austin gets in your face, which he will before tonight ends, you have a real answer."

I frown, shifting my gaze toward Austin. He happens to look up at the same moment and when our eyes meet, he stares at me with an uncertainty I've never detected from him before. Shit. Torsten's right. This whole night, I've been so wrapped up in Indy, in her energy and connection, that I've dismissed all the looks we've been getting.

After things with Courtney went sideways, I decided I'm living my life for me and I don't give a shit who is or isn't watching. But maybe Indy doesn't want all that attention, all that poking into her business. Maybe I've unknowingly placed her in a position she doesn't want to be in.

I've done it all by being careless and not having the decency to talk to her first.

But what the hell am I going to say? *I'm desperate when I'm around you but I don't know what that means.* Blowing out an exhale, I drain my drink and place it on the bar.

"I should talk to Indy," I mutter to Torsten who looks surprised by my statement.

He nods once, serious. "Okay."

"I'm going to find her." I tip my head toward Austin. "Keep him occupied, will ya?"

Torsten snorts. "Yeah, man."

I smack the back of my hand against his shoulder as I stride toward the bathrooms. Posting up outside the women's room, I'm relieved that the bathrooms are part of the private room and not for general use. It means no one bothers me and the wait is relatively short.

Three minutes barely pass before Indy waltzes out the door, giggling with her cousins like schoolgirls. All their laughter dies as they spot me, their eyes simultaneously widening.

I chuckle. "You look like a bunch of schoolgirls."

Vanny grins. "I'm taking that as a compliment, Scotch. I'm almost thirty-four." She grabs Claire's arm and begins to steer her away.

"Can we talk?" I ask Indy.

She shoots her cousins a desperate look but they glance between us and scurry away, their laughter ringing out before they clear the hallway.

Indy shuffles from one foot to the other, looking at me for clues.

I hold out a hand and she tentatively takes it. I pull her around the corner of the hallway where there's a small alcove. Her eyes dart around the mostly private space before finding mine.

"Is everything okay?" she asks.

The corners of my mouth tug up. God, she's so endearing. So innocent and cute and too damn good for a guy like me. "Indy, I didn't mean to put you on blast by being handsy at the bar."

She frowns. "Handsy?"

I nod. "Can't keep my hands off you. But with so many people around and your family"—I shrug, stuffing my hands into my pockets to keep them from reaching for her—"I shouldn't have put you in that position. Especially without talking to you first."

She looks wary, her lips pressing into a thin line. "And this is you talking to me about it?"

I bite the corner of my mouth, unable to reach her thoughts, or get a feel for this situation at all. Twenty minutes ago, this girl's ass was pressed against my dick and now, she's looking at me like she wants to slap me. "This is me making sure I didn't blow up your spot when you don't want everyone to know we're hooking up. I don't give a fuck what anyone out there thinks. To be honest, I don't even give a shit if I'm pissing Austin off. But it's not fair to have all this attention thrown on you without knowing if you want it or not."

Her frown deepens and confusion ripples over her expression. "I don't understand what you're saying. Are you into me or not?" she asks point-blank.

My mouth drops open. She can't tell if I'm into her? Jesus Christ, I am fucking this up. Maybe this is why Courtney and I didn't work out, maybe I really am an idiot when it comes to emotional intelligence.

Indy shifts her weight, her cheeks turning pink as she averts her gaze.

Not overthinking it, I pull my hands from my pockets. We're in a private space with no peeking eyes to worry about.

I stride toward her and she looks up, surprised. She backs up until her back presses into the wall and I'm in front of her, my hands wrapping around her waist. I look down into her bright green eyes, wondering how I ever thought I could not act on my feelings for her. They're more than just lust, than just this moment. The realization should scare me after the shit Courtney put me through this year. But I don't feel frightened. Instead, I feel excited. Invigorated and validated and fucking happy.

"Little Indy, I can't keep my hands off you. I'm so into you that I want to kiss you senseless and take you home with me and keep you in my bed. I want to take you out for dinner this Saturday and spend all day Sunday doing touristy shit with you again in Boston."

Her eyes widen and her mouth falls open, a startled breath dropping from her lips.

I smile. "But you have a full day of classes and a trip that you're planning. We're friends and I just started the season and you don't date hockey players. My life is messy and most of it is in the public eye. I want whatever you're willing to give me and more but not at the expense of your commitments to yourself."

Her eyes scan my face, dropping to my lips, coming back to my eyes, and falling to my mouth again.

Before I can ask her what she wants, she pushes up on her tippy toes and kisses me. Her mouth is sweet and spicy, raspberries and tequila. Hot and cold, sunshine and snowflakes. Her hands grip the tops of my shoulders as she falls into me, her mouth gentle for one single kiss before her tongue dips into my mouth and my entire body comes to life.

I growl, pressing her back against the wall as I slant my mouth over hers and meet her kiss for kiss. In seconds, our kiss turns hungry, needy, borderline desperate. My hand cups her cheeks to hold her head steady as I deepen our connection. She whimpers, our panting filling the silence of the small space.

I pull back, gazing down at her.

Her eyes are glowing, her cheeks flushed. She's so fucking gorgeous. A swell of protectiveness surges through my body, making me swear. I'd want to knock out anyone, any guy on my team, who ever saw her looking the way she is right now. Her eyes are wide, her hair wild from where my fingers ran through it. She's rocking the sexiest bedroom eyes I've ever seen and the only thing I can think about is getting us out of here and somewhere more private. Like my bedroom. Or her apartment.

"Tell me what you want, Indiana?" My voice is husky. Ragged.

She smirks, still clinging to that edge of sass. "Take me home, Noah. Quick, before anyone realizes we're missing."

I grin, licking my bottom lip. Lacing our fingers together, I drop my forehead to hers. "Indy, if we bolt, we're outing ourselves to the team. To your cousins. Are you sure about this?"

She shakes her head. "I haven't been sure about anything since you came back into my life, Noah."

That causes a flare of uncertainty to spark in my chest.

Indy smiles. "But I like it. This. Feeling instead of thinking all the damn time."

I kiss the corner of her mouth and pull back. Grabbing my phone from my back pocket, I shoot off a message to my driver and one to Torsten. Jesse replies that he's waiting out back for us. Torsten sends me a string of emojis I can't fucking decipher.

"Come on." I pull her toward the back exit. "Jesse, my

driver, is waiting for us here. Message Claire and Savannah so they know where you are."

"And Austin?" she asks, her expression playful.

"Not going there tonight, babe. Not when I can enjoy my time with you."

She laughs and follows me out into the blustering cold. "I'll make sure my cousins grab our coats."

I bundle her under my arm as we race to the car. Pulling open the backdoor, we both slide inside. I grin, feeling like we're pulling off some kind of a secret mission instead of being two adults heading home together.

That's the thing with Indy, she injects light into everything. With her, even the mundane is thrilling. "That would be good," I agree, turning toward Jesse. "Hey Jes."

"Hey man. Good game tonight."

"Thanks. My house, please."

"You got it." He eases the car toward the street and turns up the volume on the *Hamilton* soundtrack he's listening to.

I glance over at Indy who's smiling at me. I grin back, knowing we're both being goofy and silly.

But it feels right. Being with her feels good.

And there's no way in hell I'm questioning that. Not when I've got Indy beside me, her hand in mine.

17

INDY

A s soon as the door to Noah's brownstone clicks closed, the reality of the situation descends over me. I'm in Noah's home again. But this time, it's different.

I know it. He knows it. And the realization makes the moment seem significant. If I take this step with Noah, it's going to be more than just casual. More than just a fling. I don't know how to do casual well to begin with but clearly, I really don't know how to do casual with a man like Noah. A hockey player. A sweet talker. A heartthrob who makes my body burn with one smoldering glance.

Jesus. I falter, my breath stuttering in my chest as I acknowledge just how much I *like* Noah.

Already, in the span of a few weeks, my feelings for him are real and complicated. I feel too many things in his presence, want too many things for the future that I know I shouldn't.

He steps toward me, his fingers gripping my chin and tilting my face until I meet his eyes. "What is it? What's wrong?"

Panic grips me for a second as I drown in the dark pool of

his gaze. He's already too much. This is too much. And the last time I let myself go there, it ended with my self-confidence shredded and my heart shattered. "You're making me break all my rules," I whisper, my eyes pleading with him to understand. The Indy I've been since I've met Noah again, the Indy I am when I'm in his company, is so different than the woman I've been for the past five years. The thing is, I really like her. But can I be her without Noah in my life?

What if things between us go sideways?

What if they don't?

The thoughts collide in my head, warring for consideration.

"I'm not trying to change you, Indy," he swears, his face pained at the thought.

"It's not that. It's that I like who I am when I'm with you."

"Then what's the problem?"

"What if things go badly between us?"

"Why do you think that?" he asks, more curious than hurt.

I shrug. "You're a professional hockey player."

"You're a professor."

I smirk. "You travel a lot."

"You don't."

"Noah!"

He grins, brushing some of my hair out of my eyes. "Babe, none of those details matter. I like you. You like me. Things between us are good, fun. But if this is too much, if you're not feeling me or this or whatever, then say it. If you want to leave right now, I'll take you home. We'll be friends and we'll be cool. The only thing I don't want you to do is make a decision you'll regret." He scrapes his teeth over his bottom lip, shaking his head. In a lower voice, he adds, "I don't know if I could handle you regretting me, Indy."

I swallow, mentally weighing the pros and cons. Suddenly, it all seems like too much. My racing thoughts, my knotted stomach, my desperate heart. Should I just tell him my feelings for him are *more* than casual? That even though I said I could do this, I was wrong? But if I tell him, will I lose everything I share with him? The thought makes me feel nauseous and unsteady.

"Tell me what you're thinking, Indy."

I open my mouth. On the tip of my tongue are a thousand confessions. Truths that resonate in every fiber of my being but something holds me back from saying them aloud.

I glance up into Noah's chocolate eyes and concerned expression. I clear my throat. *Just say it, Indy. Own it.* He frowns, his hands cupping my cheeks. He peers at me with such intensity that I...chicken out. What if I scare him away?

I shake my head and force a smile. "I want to stay, Noah."

He studies me for a long beat. "You sure?"

I nod, leaning toward him.

I don't have to lean far because Noah closes the gap, wrapping me in his arms and dropping his mouth to mine. My eyes flutter closed as I fall into the heady sensations his touch provides. His kiss is hot and passionate. He intoxicates me as his scent wraps around me and his touch drags me under. Ripping his mouth from mine, he trails kisses down my neck and I moan, arching my back to give him more access.

His mouth on my skin sparks something deep inside of me. Wildfire flares through my veins as my thoughts blur and the only thing I can focus on is how damn good my body feels under his touch. Easily, as if I weigh nothing, Noah picks me up and my legs wind around his hips. His mouth never leaves my skin as he carries me up the stairs and to his bedroom. When we enter the room, he places me in the center of his bed and pulls back several paces, staring at me. Hesitation flickers across his expression and my anxiety flares to life.

"What's wrong?" I ask.

"Absolutely nothing." He shakes his head, tugging his sweater over his head with one hand, the way he always does. He drops it to the floor and my eyes zero in on his defined abs. "I like how you look in my bed." Noah grins, losing his jeans. He moves to the edge of the mattress and leans over me, placing a sloppy kiss on my lips.

I lie back until my head hits the mattress and Noah climbs over me, straddling my waist. He brushes my hair out of my eyes and gazes at me as if he's memorizing my face.

I blush and he grins.

"Little Indy, what are you doing to me?" he murmurs, leaning forward to press a kiss against my left cheek, followed by my right, followed by my forehead, the corners of my mouth, and finally my lips.

By the time his lips brush against mine, I'm practically vibrating with need. No man but him has ever taken their time with me and the buildup makes me feel off-balance. I arch my back, pressing into Noah as his tongue fills my mouth. While he kisses me, his fingers deftly pop the buttons on my sweater until it hangs open, with just my black bra between us.

He makes a sound in the back of his throat as his hand cups my breast, squeezing gently. Then his mouth leaves mine as he zeros in on his hand, his fingers teasing my nipple.

I can't tear my gaze away as Noah's fingers brush across my nipple, tweaking once, twice, three times, before gently peeling back the cup of my bra. My nipple tingles against the cool air, tight and peaked and a dusty pink. Noah licks his lips, his gaze shooting to mine. "You're fucking perfect, Indy," he says, his voice rough, before dipping his head and slowly dragging his tongue around and over my nipple.

I shudder and his hand begins to work my other breast as his mouth fastens against the nipple on display, teasing and sucking until I drop my head back, moaning. Noah removes my sweater and bra entirely and lavishes my breasts with enough attention that heat pools in my center and my hips start involuntarily pressing up, searching for him, for the delicious friction I know he can provide.

But he doesn't hurry. Instead, he takes his time, kissing my skin, swirling his tongue around my belly button, caressing my jean-clad inner thighs with his long fingers. Everything about tonight feels different. There's a languidness to our connection when it's always seemed desperate. Tonight, we're savoring instead of sprinting and with each passing moment, I fall more under Noah's spell.

Slowly, he unbuttons my jeans and drags down the zipper, his breath catching as he spots the black and hot pink thong I'm wearing. "These are sexy, baby." He runs his fingers featherlight over the lace and I squirm.

He does it again, grinning at me. "Are you wet for me?"

I nod, licking my lips. Part of me knows his words should embarrass me. No man has ever spoken to me so boldly before. But I'm too turned on, too desperate for his touch, to care. He works my jeans over my hips and I hear them hit the floor. Noah pauses, hooking one of my legs over his shoulder and nipping at the inside of my thigh.

He licks his lips, as if his mouth is watering and I feel my core clench in anticipation. Dropping his head, he presses open-mouthed kisses against my thighs as his fingers slide over the material of my thong and the pad of his thumb swipes down my center.

I shudder and he swears, doing it again. "So wet for me,

baby." His voice is strained as he takes two fingers and circles them over my clit, featherlight at first but working into a rhythm that has my hips bucking off the mattress and my eyes squeezing closed.

"So beautiful," he murmurs before I feel his hot tongue against my core. Holy shit. He shifts his weight, his tongue replacing his fingers against my clit as two of his fingers enter me.

"Oh God," I moan, my hands clutching at my breasts as Noah works me into an inferno, with my body trembling for release.

"I got you, Indy." His voice is caressing before I feel his mouth on me again. Hot, passionate, and sexy, Noah's sounds mix with mine, coloring the air with the scent of arousal and need.

He builds my body up in increments until everything inside of me tightens and explodes, and I cry out, riding the most powerful wave I've ever experienced. "Noah!"

He slows his mouth and fingers but continues to work me over until the last tremble recedes from my body.

Jesus. I can't move. I can't open my eyes. I can't even think.

"Fucking gorgeous," Noah murmurs, kissing my hip. "And you taste like candy. Sweet."

I force my eyes open and nearly gasp at the expression on his face. It's filled with wonder and a little bit of bewilderment. He moves up my body, positioning himself at my entrance. I feel the tip of him press against me and I shudder.

"Condom?" I squeak out, my voice husky, my body still trembling. This time, in need for him. For more.

He pauses, reaching over to grab one from his bedside table. Noah swears, dropping his forehead to mine. "We burned through that box, babe. Shit, I forgot to buy more."

I groan, closing my eyes. I've never not used a condom before, not even with Jace. I've been on the pill for years and know that I'm clean but a condom always provided an added layer of protection.

"I'm sorry, Indy," Noah sighs, starting to pull away.

My hips angle up, searching for him. For the first time since we started this thing, jealousy rises in my throat. I try not to think of all the women who have been in his bed before me to warrant keeping a jumbo box of condoms on hand but I can't squash the flicker of envy. Obviously, I know he's been with a hell of a lot of women. But does he light all of them up like that? Has he ever skipped on using a condom before?

"I'm on the pill," I rasp out. "And I'm clean."

"So am I," Noah murmurs, his eyes searching mine. "You sure about this, Indy?" he stalls, reading something in my expression.

I nod.

He hesitates, waiting me out.

"Everything with you is more intense," I admit. "It's never been like this for me before."

He gazes down at my naked body and back to my face. "Ever?"

I shake my head.

"Good. I've never enjoyed making a woman come apart the way I do you, baby." He brushes my hair back from my forehead. "Fucking desperate to get inside you, Indy. Thought about this since I looked up at the game and saw you sitting in the box. But we don't have to do—"

"I want to," I cut him off.

Noah brushes a kiss over my lips before pushing my knees up to my sides. He lines up at my entrance. Glancing at me, he slides inside and my eyes roll back in my head. For the first time ever, there's nothing between us and it feels incredible.

"Fuck, you feel like heaven, Indy." His voice is strained as he slides back before pushing into me again.

I force my eyes open, holding his gaze. His eyes are darker than midnight but something new shimmers around the edges.

"Tell me what you want, Little Indy."

"Make me feel everything, Noah."

He drops down and swipes a kiss across my mouth. "It'd be my pleasure, baby."

He gives me everything and more. As his mouth takes mine and he works a steady rhythm between us, my body craves his. For the first time ever, I think I truly understand addiction.

I'll never get enough of Noah Scotch.

Not when he makes my body tighten and shatter.

Not when he makes my skin ache and shiver.

Not when he makes my mind simultaneously quiet and overflow.

And definitely not when he makes my heart flutter and yearn.

I cry out again with Noah swearing my name shortly afterwards.

As I come down from the greatest sex I've ever had in my life, fear fills my stomach. Now that Noah is in my life, I know it will never be the same again.

But how long will he stick around for?

18

NOAH

I've been waking up with Indiana in my bed for weeks now, but today, it feels different. In a good way. But still, I don't know what the hell to make of it.

When she rolls over and I feel her warmth press into my skin, my hands want to slide over her curves and claim her all over again. The realization settles like a stone in my stomach. This is not me. With most morning-afters, I'm out of bed and out for a run with the sunrise. With Indy, I'm up, showered, and popping a Nespresso pod into the machine. But this morning, I don't make a move to do any of those things.

And I definitely never say shit like, "Hey, want to grab brunch?"

Indy rubs the sleep from her eyes, her hair spread over my pillow like a fan. "I love brunch."

Of course she does. She loves everything and being with her is as easy as breathing. I don't even have to think about it.

"I know a place," I say instead, pulling myself from the cocoon of blankets we wrapped ourselves in last night, sheltered from the world. A time-out that let me focus on the feel of Indy's long legs wrapped around my torso and the sweet sounds that fall from her lips instead of the away game I have this week in Cleveland.

"Cool." She throws off the comforter and swipes her purse off the floor. The bathroom door closes several minutes later and I let out a long exhale.

Bracing my elbows against my knees, I drop my head in my hands and try to regroup. Last night was fun. It was hot. It was fucking sexy as hell; Indy's sexy as hell. But it was also different from any of the other times we've hooked up. Something between us shifted. Something changed.

But what?

This morning, Indy seems fine. She's not acting weird or clingy or anything. In fact, she seems to be a hell of a lot cooler than me.

I hear the toilet flush and the faucet turn on. Several minutes later, Indy pulls open the door. Her face is bare, her hair pulled into a messy bun. She's wearing her jeans from last night and buttoning up the sweater that I wanted to rip off of her body all night. She doesn't look like she's doing a walk of shame. She doesn't look nervous. She just looks…normal.

I stand and pull a pair of sweats and a hoodie from my dresser. "It's just around the corner."

"Sounds good." She smiles, sliding the strap of her purse over her shoulder. "Ah, wait, I left my coat at the bar last night."

"I got you, babe." I bundle her up in one of my thicker hoodies, liking the way it looks hitting her mid-thigh. I roll the sleeves up on her arms, grinning at how damn adorable she looks. And how much I like seeing her rock my number.

We head outside and I tuck Indy under my arm as the cold wind whips against us. Everything between us screams more than "just friends" and yet, I can't bring myself to bring it up.

Our arrangement is easy. It's working. It's fun and I like

hanging out with her. Why the hell would I rock the boat now?

I guide her toward the restaurant. The wind makes talking nearly impossible so we hustle along in silence. Once we're tucked into a back booth, Indy slides off my hoodie and moans when the server drops a carafe of coffee on our table.

I grin.

"What?" She raises an eyebrow, pouring our coffees. "You kept me up late. The need for caffeine is real."

I chuckle, nudging the cream closer to her. "It was worth it."

She nods coyly, lifting her mug toward mine and clinking it in cheers. "Definitely worth it."

"Indy, you are the coolest girl I know," I tell her, taking a sip of the hot coffee.

"What do you mean?"

"Just, God, any other girl would have a million and one expectations after these past few weeks." I clear my throat, not knowing how to address all the thoughts swirling in my mind. "Especially after last night," I tack on, wanting to feel her out. Did she feel the shift between us too? Was there even a shift if only one of us felt it? "But you, you're just—"

"Normal."

"Chill," I settle on. "I like how much fun we have together without all the drama bullshit."

She bites her bottom lip, a strand of uncertainty rippling over her face, before she nods. I frown, wondering if I've offended her. I lean forward and touch her wrist but before I can say anything, she says, "I know what you mean. The only other time I tried casual, the guy, Chris, had all of these other ideas and assumptions and it sort of ruined our time together."

Well, that sours my mood. "Chris?" I ask, wondering who the hell he is.

She wrinkles her nose and nods. "It was right before I moved here. It was stupid; we knew it wouldn't amount to anything. My best friend found the whole thing highly entertaining, especially after Chris insinuated he would visit Boston." She rolls her eyes.

I swallow, sliding my hand back across the table. Of course Indy dated and had relationships, serious and not. Six months ago, I was going to walk down the damn aisle. Still, it stings to think of her with other men. In fact, it bothers me more than thinking of Courtney with her lawyer husband.

That realization is unsettling and I sit back in my chair, the weight of the morning coming down on my shoulders. What the hell is going on?

The server appears to take our order and I breathe out a sigh of relief. Indy orders French toast, I ask for whole grain pancakes, and we both pick up our coffee mugs.

I glance at Indy over the rim of my mug. Her green eyes are bright and glittery. She stares back with a coy smile playing over her lips.

When I place down my coffee mug, she laughs and I lean forward again, desperate to know whatever is going on in her head.

"Noah," she says.

I nod.

She gestures between us. "I know we don't normally do this type of thing."

I frown. "Eat?"

She rolls her eyes. "Morning-after breakfast."

I bite my tongue, both wanting and not wanting to know what she's going to say because somehow, I feel like it's going to change things. And I'm not sure if I want things to change or stay exactly how they are. I mean, they're good, right? I clear my throat. "I promised to show you the other side of Boston."

She lifts an eyebrow. "Is this it?" She glances around the quiet restaurant, a far cry from the bustling brunch scene over in Back Bay.

Still, her expression breaks some of the ice forming in my chest and I let out a chuckle. Placing my palms up, I tip my head in acknowledgement. "All right, Little Indy, you got me. This wasn't my best show of Boston's brunch scene."

She snorts, leaning closer until the table cuts into her chest. The soft swell of her breasts push up underneath her sweater and I remember the way they fit so perfectly in my hands last night.

I drag my gaze back up to her eyes. Indy shoots me an amused look but her eyes flare with heat and I realize why I don't do morning brunch with Indy. She's too goddamn tempting.

Our server drops off our breakfast dishes and Indy's face lights up like a little kid at Christmas. She cuts into her French toast, moaning appreciatively. I stare at her.

How the hell did this happen? Of course I knew from the moment I saw her again that I was drawn to her. I can admit that she's gorgeous, intelligent, quick, and funny.

After Courtney, I never expected to feel so much for another woman in such a short amount of time. If I'm being honest with myself, things with Indy are completely different than they were with Courtney. In some ways, I already feel more for Indy, want more with her.

How long can we keep doing this delicate dance before one of us gets hurt?

I told Indy to be straight with me but here I am, watching

her eat French toast like she's a marvel of the modern world. Who's the one not being straight now?

I don't date hockey players.

For the first time since Indy dropped that detail, it bothers me. I used to think those were the greatest words she could have told me.

Now, I really wish she'd amend them and tell me something else entirely.

19

INDY

"You look exhausted," Claire comments as I unwind my scarf from around my neck.

I groan, hanging my coat in the hall closet. "I am. I've been fighting a sore throat and sinuses." I throw my hand in the air. "I always get like this during midterms. I just started a Z-pack." Claire shoots me a sympathetic look and I force a smile. "But I do love this time of year."

"Thanksgiving was always your favorite." Aunt Mary leans in to kiss me hello but I shoo her away.

"I'm fighting something," I explain.

She wraps an arm around my shoulder anyway. "You work too hard, Indy. You need to take care of yourself. You've been so busy lately, we've hardly seen you."

"Busy getting some d," my cousin mutters and I shoot her a murderous glare.

Luckily, Aunt Mary doesn't hear her.

"I've just been working a lot. We are flying out in six weeks for the trip to Bangladesh. With all the Thanksgiving plans—"

"And Friendsgiving plans," Claire adds.

"And Friendsgiving plans"—I roll my eyes at my cousin, who roped me into a wine and charcuterie night with her and Rielle—"I've been trying to get things sorted before the long weekend. Besides, I have another dinner with my department this week."

"Oh, that's fun." Aunt Mary's eyes glitter. "Are you taking a special someone?" She guides me toward the kitchen but I hear Claire's snickering behind us.

"Uh…not planning on it." I accept a mug of hot cocoa from my uncle as he kisses the top of my head in greeting.

"Really?" Aunt Mary presses. "I could have sworn you were seeing someone, Indy. You've been busier than 'just work busy.'"

Claire covers her laughter by coughing into her hand.

"You really shouldn't wear yourself out by working all the time. You need fun too. A social outlet. You should invite someone to your dinner this week," Aunt Mary says firmly as Austin and Noah round the corner into the kitchen.

"What dinner?" Austin asks, popping a square of cheese and a cracker into his mouth.

"Indiana has a Thanksgiving dinner with her department," Aunt Mary explains, shooting me another curious look. "Don't you think she should bring a nice man? She works too much…"

A smile plays over Noah's mouth as he swipes some cheese and crackers from the board in the center of the island.

"You want me to set you up?" Austin offers, raising an eyebrow.

Noah's head snaps up and he glares at my cousin. Austin glares back.

I snort and shake my head. After sneezing into my elbow, I say, "No, thanks. I'm really all good. It's just a boring, department dinner. I'd rather not subject someone to office politics and hearing about everyone's dissertations. I'd never get another date."

Austin points at me with his mother's wine glass that he nabbed off the island. "Good point, Indy. See, you're too smart for us."

Aunt Mary sighs and takes her wine glass from Austin's outstretched hand. She pulls down more wine glasses from the cabinet as Austin pours for all of us. Moments later, my parents arrive and our usual Sunday night dinner commences.

"We're hosting Thanksgiving this year." Mom kisses me hello, beaming. Since we never lived near family when I was growing up, I know how excited she is to host a holiday.

"That's great, Mom. What can I bring?" I pass her a wine glass.

"Just yourself." Mom frowns. "You look exhausted, Indiana."

I shake my head, filling her in on my Z-pack. Mom clucks her tongue.

Noah appears at my shoulder and slips a fresh glass into my hand.

"Thanks." I smile up at him.

"Oh, you'll be joining us, won't you, Noah?" Mom asks him.

Noah furrows his brow.

"For Thanksgiving," Mom clarifies.

Noah reels back, a bit surprised I think. "Uh, sure. Thank you for the invitation, Leanne."

"Of course. You're family." Mom smiles up at him and I choke on my wine.

As I'm coughing into my elbow like a lunatic, Mom shoots me a look while Noah pats my back.

"Sorry," I recover, clearing my throat. "Wrong pipe."

Noah glances at Mom. "I'm going to visit my brother in the morning, but I can come by afterwards."

Mom beams, squeezing his forearm, before excusing herself to see if my aunt needs any help with dinner.

"You okay?" Noah asks me, his eyebrows furrowing.

I nod, forcing a smile. I can't believe my mom just invited Noah to Thanksgiving. I mean, of course she should. He's practically family and other than Easton, he wouldn't have anyone to spend the holiday with unless he went to visit his own parents who he conveniently never mentions.

But I haven't spent a holiday with a guy I'm—seeing, dating, hooking up with?—since Jace. I don't bring guys around. I keep them tucked safely in a box far away from my parents.

"I don't have to come to your parents' if it makes you uncomfortable," Noah says, correctly reading my hesitation.

"No, don't be silly. Of course you should come." I flick a wrist, feeling guilty for even *thinking* that Mom shouldn't have asked him.

Noah watches me for a long moment. "What's this dinner you've got at work?"

"Oh, that." I wrinkle my nose. "It's just a department thing. Going to be boring but I have to make an appearance."

"Of course." Noah shifts his weight.

"I'd uh, I'd invite you but it's Tuesday night," I say finally.

Noah nods, sipping his wine. "I have an away game."

"Yeah," I say, both relieved and disappointed that Noah won't be able to join me. On the one hand, it would be nice to finally have a date to one of these things. Instead of always being the usually lone single woman that all the divorced men feel the need to chat up. On the other hand, I'm not ready to mix my professional life with Noah. All the overlap of my circles causes anxiety to flare in my chest because this thing with Noah isn't for forever. Deep down, I know that. I need to stick to what we agreed on. I drain my wine glass. "Shall we?" I tip my head toward the kitchen where my aunt is calling everyone to dinner.

Noah nods but his eyes are guarded, watching me with an edge of uncertainty I don't like. Even if I put it there. Even if I need it there.

FOR THE REST of the night, things between Noah and me feel off. I don't know exactly what changed but I suddenly feel nervous around him and he seems guarded.

We keep shooting each other surreptitious glances that only heighten the anxiety I feel.

After dinner at my aunt's, Noah and I head out at the same time.

"I've got an early flight tomorrow." He pulls open the driver's side door to my car.

"I know."

He hesitates, shifting his weight from one foot to the other. "If you want to come by…"

I swallow past the lump forming in my throat, unsure if he wants me to say yes or no. "Um, it's going to be a busy week for me so…"

"I get it." He nods.

"I mean, if I don't come tonight, I won't see you 'til the weekend so," I take a deep inhale, "I'd like to come."

Relief streaks across his face and he smiles. It's genuine and it eases some of the tightness in my chest. "Come."

"Okay." I smile back. "I'll follow you."

I trail Noah to his house and once we're tucked inside the

warmth of his brownstone some of the awkwardness from dinner evaporates.

"You want a drink?" he asks over his shoulder as I follow him into the kitchen.

"No, thanks." I slide onto a barstool.

He fills a glass of water and downs it.

"What time is your flight tomorrow?" I ask, picking at a loose thread on the cuff of my sweater.

"Seven a.m."

I whistle and he grins.

"So you've got a busy week?" He leans forward over the kitchen island and I try not to be distracted by the way his shoulders roll and bunch. All muscle. All of him. It's unfair really; how could I not be distracted?

"Yep. Midterm exams before the students go home for Thanksgiving break, things to finalize for our research trip, and a holiday reception with the Political Science department."

"Sounds fun."

"Liar."

Noah chuckles and tips his head toward the stairs.

I lead the way and he swats my ass as I scurry up the stairs.

Once I'm in his bedroom, I collapse in the center of his bed. Bracing my arms behind me, I gaze up at Noah as he enters the dark room and kicks the door closed behind him. The moonlight streams through the windows, casting shadows on his face.

He stares at me with an intensity I'm unprepared for. His eyes burn with emotions I don't understand. "Indiana," he murmurs my name, and it's both a plea and a curse.

I drop to my elbows as he strides to the side of the bed.

His frame hovers over mine, his eyes boring straight to my soul.

"What's wrong?" I whisper.

He shakes his head and tugs off his shirt.

I inhale, watching as the moonlight ripples over his abdomen. He could be carved from marble, that's how breathtaking he is. He's art. His body is powerful, strong, and mesmerizing. Tenderness sweeps his expression and I gasp at the longing in his gaze. My elbows give out from underneath me and the back of my head hits his mattress. Noah climbs onto the bed and straddles me, careful to keep his weight from crushing me.

His teeth scrape over his bottom lip and he swears. "God, you're so fucking beautiful." His face hovers over mine, pleading and tortured. "What are you doing to me, Indy?" His voice is strangled and I frown, wanting to ask what he means, wanting to understand what he's asking. But before I can form a word, his lips find mine. He kisses me hard, with a torrent of unspoken emotions. I moan, arching into him as he presses into me.

His touch is hot against my skin and suddenly, it's like I can't get enough of him. A frenzy works in my blood, blocking out rational thought. My hands track his biceps, his rib cage, his hard pecs as they press into my palms. His tongue swirls down the column of my neck, his fingers making quick work of the buttons down my blouse.

When his mouth latches onto my nipple, the hot air of his breath trapped between my skin and the cup of my bra, I groan. There's nothing remarkable about this moment except that it feels like more than anything I've ever felt before. It's sexier, headier, and so much needier. Desire pools between my legs as Noah unclasps my bra and my breasts spill into his waiting hand and mouth.

He wastes no time teasing me, working my body in tiny increments that have my legs winding around his waist.

I reach for him, deftly unzipping his jeans.

"Jesus," Noah swears, kicking off his pants and pulling my leggings and underwear down in one swift tug. "Need you, baby. Fuck."

I gaze up at him, noting the rise and fall of his chest, the wild gleam in his eyes, the veins that pop along his strong forearms.

"Want you, Noah," I manage to say before he pushes into me. We both cry out and he stills, letting me adjust to him.

He gathers me to his chest, pressing kisses into my hair. "You okay?"

"Move, Noah. Please," I practically beg him.

He chuckles but it comes out as a groan as he begins to pull back and press into me.

Fuck, I see stars. Because the sensations flowing through my body aren't just physical, there's an emotional aspect I've never shared with Noah before. Each time we hook up, it's a little bit more intense, but tonight, it's a whole new level of passion. It colors the air around us, makes the space between us vibrate, and travels through my limbs like a live wire.

"So fucking good, Indy," Noah mutters, working a faster pace. He flips us so I'm sitting on top, straddling him. My palms smack the center of his chest as I begin to move and he swears loudly, throwing his head back.

Jesus, he's divine. One of the hottest men I've ever seen and the fact that I can do *this* to him is like a drug. It hits me like a shot of adrenaline, helping me find my rhythm. My one hand strays from his body and caresses my own, tweaking my nipple as Noah's eyes widen.

"That's it, Indy. Feel me, baby," he demands, guiding himself up, meeting me thrust for thrust.

But I'm too far gone to process his words. Too into this moment, into him, to understand anything other than the delicious sensations rocking through me. My desire heightens in increments that has my abdomen clenching and my thighs shaking. Noah moves forward, his hands finding my waist and guiding me up and down, up and down. Faster.

"So gorgeous, baby."

I cry out, biting my bottom lip. My hands curls around his shoulders, my nails piercing his skin. "Noah."

"Come for me, Indy. Please baby, let me see you break apart." His voice is guttural, desperate. It's my undoing.

I shatter. I break into a million tiny pieces that feel like sunshine and rain and perfection. As I ride the wave of bliss, Noah rolls me underneath him and thrusts into me at a frantic pace until he falls over the edge, calling out my name, and collapses on top of me.

We breathe in each other's breaths, both of us panting. My body feels like a puddle, my mind whipping with too many thoughts to process. But my heart, oh my heart, is straight up galloping and skipping beats.

Noah lets out a shaky exhale and slides out of me, rolling onto his back beside me.

For several moments, only the sounds of our breathing and our ricocheting thoughts fill the room.

Then, I feel Noah's hand slip over mine. "Indy?"

I turn my head a tiny bit to study his profile. "Yeah?"

"You okay?"

I nod, trying to find words to describe how I am. Because I'm better than I've ever been in my entire life. "Better than okay."

He squeezes my fingers. "Me too. You are spectacular."

I snort, liking when he's both sweet and playful. "Right back at you, Scotch."

Instead of chuckling like I expect, Noah turns toward me. His eyes are bottomless, dark and deep. He holds my gaze for a long moment and something passes between us. I don't have a word for it but it's *more*. More than just desire, than attraction, than this moment.

I clear my throat and Noah blinks. Then he slides from the bed and cleans up in the bathroom. I blow out a deep exhale and force myself to my feet even though my legs feel like jelly. My entire being feels off-balanced, as if I've lost my equilibrium and the entire world is shaky.

When Noah opens the bathroom door, he smiles at me and brushes a kiss across my lips. "I'm sorry I need to set an early alarm."

"Don't be. I know you have to leave before the sun's up." I enter the bathroom and rinse off quickly in the shower.

When I re-enter the room, Noah's soft snore fills the space. His suitcase is opened next to the bed, ready for tomorrow's flight.

I slip underneath the covers and shimmy closer to him, liking the way the warmth of his body seeps into my skin. Even though there are a million thoughts jumping around my head, my body is worn out. Within moments, I drift off to sleep.

When I wake in the morning, Noah is already gone. The pale gray light of dawn wraps around me like a blanket. Everything feels different.

20

NOAH

"What's going on, man?" my brother asks, interrupting my thoughts.

"Huh?" I ask, frowning at the screen of my phone.

East chuckles through the speaker. "Damn, you got it bad. Where's your head at? You've got a game tonight."

"I know. I'm here," I grumble. My head is all over the fucking place but I'm here.

"How's Indy?" East asks slowly.

"How are *you*? How's recovery?" I focus on the matter at hand.

East snorts and I know he's going to circle back to Indy the first chance he gets. But I don't want to talk about Indy. Because Indy is great. She's a goddamn goddess and makes me feel a million things I have no clue what the hell to do with. She's amazing and I'm annoyed. I don't want to think about her a thousand times a day. I don't want to wonder what she's up to and how her classes went. I don't want any of the complications.

Indiana Merrick is smart and motivated. She's worked her ass off to establish the life she has and what she wants—

stability—is something I can't provide. So while she's glowing, bestowing her sunshine on a bunch of college freshmen, I'm growling, pissed off at the goddamn world.

Easton's irritating laughter breaks through my thoughts again.

"What?" I snap.

"Christ, bro. I'm okay, all right? I'm hanging in there. But you, you're spiraling. Trust me, I know the signs."

I swear at him.

"What's going on with Indy?"

"Nothing."

"I don't believe you," Easton taunts, singsongy.

I pinch the bridge of my nose, exasperated. "She's amazing, okay?"

Easton stops laughing. "Dude, what the hell is going on?"

I sit down on the edge of the bed in my hotel room. "We're playing Vancouver tonight."

"Yeah?"

"Fucking Jace Edwards," I spit out, my irritation spiking just thinking about seeing the asshole who hurt Indy years ago. Who made her swear off hockey players and the uncertain lifestyle we fling ourselves into, the one with no guarantees, and therefore, made her unattainable for guys like me. For me.

"Noah, did something happen with Indiana? Is she okay?" The concern in my brother's voice makes me realize how much my bitter and random rambling is messing with him.

Shit, pull it together, Scotch.

"She's fine, Easton. I just, I really like her," I admit.

"Good."

"Good?"

"Yeah, man. Why shouldn't you *like* someone? BTW, I love the middle school throwback."

I snort.

"What's the problem, Noah?" East presses.

"She came home with me last night. It was *different*."

"Different," my brother repeats, a heavy dose of skepticism in his tone.

"Different good," I hurry to add. "I think. I don't know, East, my head is all over the place. It was just great, more, something...shifted. And now, I can't get her out of my head and she's totally normal. Like, completely fine being friends who hook up while I want to pick a fight with her goddamn ex-boyfriend just because years ago, he had her."

East is quiet for several seconds. Then, a muttered, "Damn," travels through the line. "Noah, you're really into Little Indy."

"I know," I sigh, hating this. Why the hell do I have to have feelings for the one girl I can't really have? I mean, sure, I can have her. But I don't deserve her. I shouldn't want her. The only thing a guy like me offers to a woman like Indy are complications, instability, and at some point, resentment.

"Why don't you talk to her?" my brother asks slowly, trying to keep his voice neutral.

I stand from the bed again, energy bursting though my limbs. "I can't, man. She was really clear about what she wanted, what her expectations are. We both were. And now, what? I'm going to flip the script on her, take back all the things I said because she's fucking amazing? It will just mess with her head, or make things weird between us, and I don't want to do either of those things."

"Yeah, but, isn't she going to figure out you're acting strange? I mean, you're checked out, Noah. You've got three big games on the horizon and your head is in fucking la-la land over a woman you're not even going to make yours."

Not going to make yours.

That's a damn bitter pill to swallow.

I swear. Because, fuck, my brother is right. I can't make Indy mine, not the way I want to. Not when she deserves the moon and the stars and I can only give her a damn asteroid. Besides, I do need to get my head in the game. Literally. Hockey isn't a guarantee. My spot on the Hawks isn't a sure thing, neither is Easton's. Look what's happening to Torsten.

Jesus. I can't let myself spin out like this. I swore after Courtney, I was going to put hockey before everything. Look at me. I'm freaking out over a woman, at least I know she's *the* woman, but it's not going to happen and I know that too.

"I need to let her go," I murmur.

"What?" East asks.

"I'm going to her house for Thanksgiving."

"You're going to a family dinner at a woman's house?" Easton's tone is hushed.

"She's still a Merrick," I point out.

"Yeah, but one you've been inside of."

I cringe at his vulgarity. "I need to talk to her. Ease things between us. We spend too much time together. We're falling into this, this dating, when we're supposed to be casual. She needs to go on a date."

My brother laughs but when I don't join in, he stops.

"That's a terrible, awful, dumb idea."

"Thanks, East."

"Noah, I'm serious. Just…talk to her. Two minutes ago, you wanted to hit Edwards because he dated Indy in college. Now, you want to set her up?"

"I have to," I say, turning the idea over in my mind. Damn, it will gut me. Piss me off. Hurt. But it's for the best. It's what's best for her. I care about Indy and as a man who wants her to have the life she wants, I know she needs a guy who's nothing like me. She needs someone who shares her interests, who has a stable career, who might not be living across the country next year.

"Noah, think about what you're saying," Easton admonishes me.

"I have." I nod as if to emphasize the decision to myself. "This is what's best for Indy. I gotta do right by her, East."

I EAT those words six hours later when my fist connects with Jace Edwards' jaw.

Shit. I pull back, shaking out my hand.

"Are you out of your fucking mind?" Edwards cups his face.

Torsten skates in between us and angles his body in front of mine. "Fuck off, Edwards. You're lucky you're even playing tonight."

A true testament to Edwards' character is that only one of his teammates tries to insert himself in our brawl and I think it's more out of obligation than friendship.

I flip my chin to the kid, a young guy who was picked up by Vancouver this season, and back off.

"You good?" Torsten skates beside me as whistles chirp in the background.

I nod, scraping a hand over my face. I shouldn't have punched him. I know it. But when that fucker looked at me and grinned, yelling too fucking loudly "Heard you're tasting my leftovers. Who knew you liked sloppy seconds?" I lost it.

First off, how the hell does he even know about Indy and me? I know it's a small world and all that but my team is discreet. I haven't even addressed Austin about my relationship, or lack thereof, with his cousin. Second, Jace had it coming, he's had it coming for years, and I'm just the first who decided to do something about his incessant chirping. For a player who rarely sees the ice, he should watch his words. Austin slaps me on the back and I don't miss the wariness in his expression.

"He had it coming," I say by way of explanation.

"Scotch!" Coach Phillips bellows, his look incredulous.

The ref tosses me in the penalty box for five minutes.

"Damn," I mutter, skating to the box and jumping in. I'm an idiot. Even though I don't regret, not for one second, punching Edwards, I do regret that my outburst let the team down.

I swear, running a hand over my face. My bad mood darkens the longer I sit out of play and watch my team carry on with one man down. The second my time is up, I throw myself back in the game and play hard. Adrenaline burns in my veins, my head throbs, and a thinly veiled coat of anger tinges everything in my vision.

We win the game, which marginally improves my mood.

"What the hell happened out there?" Austin asks as we file out of the visitors' locker room and head for the team bus.

I shake my head. "He mouthed off."

"So?"

"So." I glare at my friend. "He said a bunch of shit about Indy and—"

"Indy," Austin cuts me off, his eyes widening. "What the hell is going on with you and my little cousin, Scotch?"

I stride past him, not caring that I'm being a douche. "Absolutely nothing," I holler over my shoulder.

That night, I don't join the team for drinks. I'm not in the mood for conversation and noise and puck bunnies with skintight jeans and too much eyeliner.

Instead, I rinse off in the shower, order room service, and channel surf for a movie.

My phone buzzes and I pause, glancing at where it sits in the center of the bed. It's Indy, I know it is. There's no way she would have missed hearing about my scrape with Edwards. Hell, there's a good chance she caught it on ESPN.

Sighing, I pick up the phone.

More messages populate my screen as I sit and contemplate what to tell her. What to do.

Indy: Hey, you okay?

Indy: What happened with Jace?

Indy: Congrats on the win. You looked great out there.

Indy: I'm still at this department dinner. Call you when I get home.

I throw down my phone and don't bother to respond. Later, when my phone buzzes on my nightstand and the screen lights up with Indy's name, I don't answer.

Tonight, I put my feelings for Indy before the best interest of my team. Before my brother's career. I need to make every second on the ice count. I can't waste time fighting nobodies like Edwards. I can't spend every second twisted up over Indiana Merrick. Not when we don't even have a future. Not when she'll always be out of my league.

I toss and turn all night.

My alarm sounds early and I ignore the two missed calls and messages from Indy asking if I'm okay. Instead, I get up, get dressed, and shoulder my bag. I single onto the team bus and stare out the window, tuning out the chatter of my teammates, as we make our way to the airport. I ignore Torsten's hard looks, blow off Austin's questions, and pop in my earbuds.

When we land in Boston, I head straight to my home and throw myself into my bed for a long sleep. Tomorrow is Thanksgiving and while I know I have a lot to be thankful for, I'm not feeling much gratitude at the moment.

Because tomorrow, I need to let Indy go. I need to make sure she understands that we broke our own rules, that we're making things between us more than what they should be. I need to cut her loose and wish her well and watch as she moves on, dating and flirting with men who aren't me.

And I need to fucking smile and nod and act like I'm not bleeding out inside.

I close my eyes and am relieved when sleep claims me.

21

INDY

Thanksgiving is hands-down my favorite holiday. Most people choose Christmas but I love Thanksgiving. I like the gratitude underlining it, I like the gatherings, and I really love yams with marshmallows, pumpkin pie, and stuffing.

Plus, being in New England this time of year adds to the allure of the holiday. It's beautiful. Really beautiful. The kind of beauty you see on postcards and wonder if it's real or not. The leaves that line the trees are deep golden, wine red, and burnt orange. The cold wind makes for rosy cheeks and perfect sweater weather. The blue sky is endless, sprinkled with fluffy clouds. It's simply exquisite.

But this Thanksgiving, my chill vibes are jittery. I'm nervous that Noah's coming. Although part of me questions if he is still coming. After he punched Jace at last night's game, I haven't heard from him. He's ignored my messages and calls and if I didn't hear from Claire that Noah and the team are fine, I'd be worried. Instead, my feelings are hurt.

"Happy Thanksgiving!" I greet Aunt Mary and Uncle Joe as I pull open the front door of my parents' home.

"Happy Thanksgiving, Indy." Aunt Mary kisses my cheek hello.

"How's the turkey coming?" Uncle Joe asks as he takes my aunt's coat from her shoulders.

"Dad hasn't messed it up yet," I inform him.

"There's still time." He grimaces and hurries to the kitchen.

I laugh as my aunt rolls her eyes. "I'm sorry Vanny couldn't come."

Aunt Mary shrugs, giving me a soft smile. "Me too. I miss her. But, such is life. She should spend the day with Mike's family. We get them for Christmas, you know?"

I laugh again. "Yeah. Are Claire and Austin nearby?"

"Oh, yes. They just went to pick up Noah. It was so thoughtful of your mom to invite him." Aunt Mary gives me a knowing glance that I try not to read into.

My mom enters the foyer and whisks Aunt Mary away with the promise of wine. The doorbell rings again. I take a deep breath and smooth down my dress over my thighs. Glancing at myself in the mirror near the door, I take in my appearance. I took extra care this morning, curling my hair, applying eyeliner and two coats of mascara. I'm wearing a high-necked, long-sleeved dress with tights and boots and while it's not the sexiest thing in the world, it's me.

I stride to the door and pull it open. "Happy Thanksgiving!"

Austin grins, Claire rolls her eyes and calls me a dork, and Noah stares at me like he's never seen me before. His expression is tight, severe. His posture is stiff. But his eyes, they bleed with emotions I don't understand and a wariness I don't like. My stomach drops and my nerves intensify. What happened in the past forty-eight hours that I missed?

"Come on in," I say, ushering them out of the cold.

My cousins kiss my cheek, pass me their coats, and set off for the kitchen but Noah hovers.

"I can take your coat." I hold out my hand.

He shrugs out of it and passes me his wool coat, his eyes intense as he studies me. "I'm sorry I didn't call you back last night."

I shrug, glancing at him over my shoulder as I place the last coat in the closet. *Give him the benefit of the doubt. Give him the chance to explain.* "I figured you passed out." I keep my voice light. Friendly.

He nods, his mouth pressed into a line.

"Congrats on the win," I add.

He snorts, the sound derisive. "Yeah, thanks."

I close the closet door and turn to face him, crossing my arms over my chest. I don't know why I feel defensive and on edge but I do. Almost like a blow is coming and I need to protect myself from its force. "What happened with Jace?"

Noah winces, shaking his head. "Nothing. It was stupid. I"—he clears his throat, his eyes blazing—"overreacted."

I bite my bottom lip, wondering if he's going to say more. He doesn't and the silence hovers between us, strained. But not strained with sexual tension and heat. Nope, this time, it feels all wrong. There's an edge to Noah I don't understand, there's a coldness in his expression, an anger in his tone. "Is everything okay?" I ask, my stomach roiling. Something is wrong but what caused it?

He stares at me, his lips fluttering like he's trying to form words but doesn't want to say them aloud.

A flare of concern fans in my stomach. Did something happen? Is Easton okay? I'm about to ask him when the doorbell rings again. I hold up one finger to Noah as I spin around and pull the door open. "Happy Thanksgiving!"

"Happy Thanksgiving, beautiful." My oldest childhood

friend, my best friend, Aiden is standing on the porch, holding a gorgeous bouquet of fall flowers.

"Aiden!" I shriek, flinging my arms around him. "What are you doing here? I mean, welcome. I didn't know you were coming."

He laughs, wrapping his arm around my waist and hugging me back, quickly moving the flowers out of the way. "Then my surprise worked." He kisses my cheek. We step inside and he hands me the flowers. "For your mom." He winks.

I grin. "With marigolds and sunflowers?"

"I know they're you're favorite," Aiden admits, adding a bottle of wine to my arms and shaking off his coat. He turns and holds out a hand to Noah. "Hey man, I'm Aiden."

Noah clears his throat, reaching forward to shake Aiden's hand. "Noah," he says coolly, his eyes narrowing.

Aiden doesn't notice Noah's coldness, probably because he's never met Noah before, but it causes me to do a double take. While I've come to know Noah as friendly, engaging, and warm, this version of him is ice cold and harsh.

"I'm going to grab a beer," Noah mutters, taking off for the kitchen.

I blink, trying to understand the shift in his behavior. Maybe something really did happen with Easton. Turning back to Aiden, I take in the big smile of my best friend and beam back. "I'm so happy to see you. When did you get into town?"

"I'm here for a conference," he explains. "It was earlier in the week but my mom told your mom and then your mom called and thought it would be a great, big surprise if I showed up for Thanksgiving dinner. That's why I didn't tell you I was coming. I wanted to surprise you. Plus, Mom and Dad are celebrating in the Caribbean this year with Marissa."

I laugh. "Tough life. Your sister was smart to move to paradise."

"Tell me about it." Aiden chuckles, wrapping his arm around my back as we set off for the kitchen. My family's loud laughter and chatter fills the house with warmth and I snuggle into my friend's side.

I haven't seen Aiden since I moved to Boston but we were neighbors in Tampa and I spent most of my childhood hanging out in his backyard and cheering on his baseball games. Not counting my cousins, he's the closest person I have to a sibling and I've missed him.

"Aiden Hardsin!" Dad exclaims as we clear the threshold. Dad drops the turkey baster and gestures for Aiden to come closer.

"It's good to see you, Mr. Jemmy," Aiden says, hugging Dad hello and using his childhood name for him.

Dad chuckles, popping the top of a beer bottle and passing it to Aiden. "Welcome to Boston. Have your toes fallen off yet?"

Aiden laughs and lifts his foot to show off his boots. "I messed up when I went for fashion over warmth."

Mom sidles up to Aiden's side and he wraps her in a hug. "Happy Thanksgiving, Lee-Lee. Indy stole your flowers."

Mom laughs and introduces Aiden to the rest of our family.

Everyone receives him warmly, like normal people. Everyone except Noah who hangs back with a scowl on his face, his eyes darting from me to Aiden and back again.

What the heck is going on with him? I lift an eyebrow but he turns away and a burst of anger blazes through me. If he's not going to talk to me and tell me what's going on, what am I supposed to do, read his mind?

Shaking my head, I busy myself by filling a vase with

water and Aiden's bouquet. Then, I pour myself a glass of wine and join the huddle around the kitchen island.

Aiden is telling a story about his first experience ice fishing and Austin is cracking up along with my dad and Uncle Joe. "I don't get it." Aiden shakes his head, placing his beer on the counter. "You literally just sit there. For hours."

Claire grins at him. "Were you by yourself?"

"That's the thing"—Aiden glances at my cousin —"Everyone is in their own little ice hut. Something about the silence and solitude. Man, the only thing I could think about is I hope my balls don't freeze off."

My family laughs and I roll my eyes, swatting Aiden on the back. He turns and smiles at me, his eyes warm and dancing with amusement. "Next time, I'm taking Indy. We all know how much she loves the outdoors."

"Good luck with that, son." Dad clasps Aiden's shoulder. "I still can't take her fishing after that time—"

"Did you see the hook in the fish?" I cut him off.

Aiden's smile widens. "How else did you think we were going to catch the fish, Indy?"

I huff, even though the memory of Aiden's and my first time fishing makes me grin. "With a net," I admit as my family's laughter swells.

Aiden wraps an arm around my shoulders and hugs me close again. "That's why you're the best, Indy. Your heart's too damn big."

"She's always been that way," Aunt Mary agrees, taking a sip of wine.

Dad brushes a kiss over the top of my head. Pockets of conversation break out as small plates are filled with the assortment of appetizers Mom spread out on the kitchen island. Wine corks are popped, beers are opened, and laughter flows as easily as the alcohol. Through it all, Noah is quiet. Reserved. Very unlike himself.

But his eyes rarely leave me and every time I catch his gaze, they're dark and desperate, brimming with a sadness I don't comprehend.

———

"Ugh, it was the worst first date ever," I groan, raising a hand to my face.

"Wait, wait. We never heard this one." Austin points at me but his eyes are on Aiden. "You gotta tell it, man."

Thanksgiving dinner was a success. Our bellies are stuffed, our cheeks are rosy, and Mom is clearing the table for dessert with Aunt Mary's help. Dad and Uncle Joe are chatting in the kitchen but the "kids" have taken over the den. For the past fifteen minutes, Aiden has been sharing embarrassing tales of my childhood with my cousins and Noah, and I've been blushing and laughing along with them.

But this story… I cut Aiden a look. "Don't."

He grins back, tugging on my hair. "But you looked so beautiful that night."

"Oh my God." I snort, pushing his shoulder. Aiden wraps his hand around my wrist and tugs me down until I'm perched in his lap.

He leans around me and gazes at Austin, Claire, and Noah. Austin and Claire look ready to burst into laughter, knowing an embarrassing story is coming. But Noah looks livid. His jaw could shatter steel and a muscle ticks in his forehead. His grip on his beer bottle is so tight, his knuckles are white. Still, he doesn't say anything, doesn't ask me if we can talk so he can tell me what the hell is going on.

By this point, I'm annoyed by his less than stellar attitude.

He's the first guy since Jace who has spent a holiday with my family. My best friend is in town visiting. Instead of being charismatic, Noah is surly. And I'm disappointed in him. As such, I look away and focus my attention on Aiden as he says the words I dread. "The afternoon of Indy's date, she insisted my brother and I include her in our baseball game."

Austin groans, knowing where this is going.

"I tried to talk her out of it. We were playing with a bunch of guys on the Varsity team and they were all pretty good. But Indy tagged along to the park, begging my brother, John, to let her play. When we got to the park, we're short a player and so John reluctantly agrees, telling her she's going to play in left field. We're in the sixth inning, the score is tied, and a beast of a guy—"

"Clarke," I say, remembering the senior with perfect clarity.

"Clarke"—Aiden nods—"steps up to the plate and hits a wicked line drive, right past the third baseman. Indy, not actually in left field but hovering around the edge of the infield picking dandelions—"

Austin snickers as Claire grins. Noah glances at me, his eyes softer than they've been all night.

"Indy looks up, wondering what all the commotion is, and the ball hits her right in the face."

"Shit," Austin says, looking at me. "Were you okay?"

I shake my head as Aiden continues. "She went down. Like, out cold. Everyone is running over to her. Someone is calling her mom. Guys are swearing, looking panicked. I slide next to her and slip my hand under her head. I'm calling her name, cradling her head in my hand, screaming at John to call Dad. And Indy's eyes flutter open and she looks right at me. Her mouth is moving but I can't hear her words so I lean closer. 'Indy,' I say, 'are you okay? Can you move?' And she

looks right at me and says, 'Aiden Hardsin, if my face is bruised for my date tonight, I'm never speaking to you again!'"

We all crack up.

"How bad was the bruise?" Claire asks me.

"She had two black eyes and an intense bump on her forehead," Aiden answers.

Austin snickers. "What'd your date say?"

I wrinkle my nose, standing from Aiden's knee. "He asked to reschedule," I say as calmly as I can while my cousins howl.

"Sounds like you guys have known each other your whole lives. Been there for everything," Noah comments after a few minutes.

"This one?" Aiden hooks his finger at me as I pick my wine glass up off the coffee table and take a sip. "She's been my best friend since I was three. We were inseparable. I went to all her damn dance recitals—"

"Hey, I came to your baseball games."

Aiden nods, polishing off his beer. "Yeah. We carpooled every morning."

"He taught me to drive stick." I snort, recalling that disaster.

Aiden grins. "I took you to prom."

"Junior prom," I clarify.

Aiden's smile dims. "Yeah, you were with that dick Edwards senior year."

I shrug, picking up the wine bottle. "It was still a fun night."

Noah's eyes track between Aiden and me as if he's trying to find some missing link. I glance at him, about to call him out and just ask what the hell his problem is today when Aiden says, "We've been through it all together. Which is why I wanted to tell you in person, Indy, that I'm moving to Boston."

My neck snaps toward his and I place down the wine bottle. A bubble of excitement swells in my chest. "What? Are you serious?"

He grins at me, nodding. "Yeah. I just got the call yesterday. I'm being transferred and well, I'll be here full-time in about two months."

"Oh my God!" I lunge myself at Aiden, throwing my arms around his neck. "This is the best news ever!"

22

NOAH

I want to punch Aiden Hardsin in the fucking face the same way I hit Jace last night.

Jesus. My hand clenches into a fist, the scrapes along my knuckles protesting. What the hell is wrong with me? Am I just going to go around beating up all the guys who got a hard-on for Indy when I'm not willing to stake a damn claim?

I can't. I can't do that to her.

And Aiden, as annoying as he is, seems like a genuinely decent guy. The kind of guy that's been looking out for Indy for the past two decades. The kind of guy who seems to hate Jace. The kind of guy that holds all her childhood moments in his mind and recalls them with perfect clarity.

I drain my beer. Bitterness and anger fill my mouth and I swipe another beer from the coffee table. In the kitchen, I hear Indy's parents and aunt and uncle talking. Out here, the fire is warming up the space as her family and *friend* sit, reminiscing. This is the life she deserves. The one where she comes home to a man like Aiden and they curl up by a fire and talk about their days, recall funny stories, and make plans for the future that they know will happen.

The realization that Indy's and my lives will never make sense the way they're supposed to, in the manner that's best for her, fills me with dread. How does she not see this? I'm watching her beam at Aiden—tall, works out, blond with blue eyes and an easy grin Aiden—who has been by her side every step of her life. They share private glances and inside jokes and so much goddamn laughter that my ears ring.

"I'm here for two weeks," Aiden continues. "And then, back to Tampa for a month and then, relocating."

"Wow!" Indy exclaims, excitement shining from her eyes like a beacon. Like Aiden just announced he cured cancer in his sleep.

Jesus, listen to me. I need to stop being so bitter. I knew from the start that we didn't have a chance; we were never supposed to have a chance. At the end of today, I was going to tell Indy that we need to pump the breaks. That things were getting too complicated, too messy. And now...yesterday's idea flickers to life in my mind and I swallow.

The perfect guy for Indy is sitting right here, looking at her with so much love and respect that my fingers curls into a fist. I open my mouth and force my idea, the one Easton warned me against, to detonate in the den.

"Indy, you should take Aiden to The Ivy next weekend," I say, relieved that my voice is even and calm. Inside, my stomach clenches and my chest burns. But on the outside, I'm cool. Controlled.

All eyes in the den turn toward me.

Indy's eyes narrow and hurt ripples over her face.

I forge ahead. "Yeah, I made reservations for Saturday night but it's not going to pan out. Why don't you guys go? You can celebrate Aiden's move. You gotta try this place, man." I turn toward Aiden as I describe the ambiance of the restaurant and their kick-ass menu. I feel Indy's glare on the side of my face but I don't turn toward her. I can't. Because I don't want to witness the disappointment in her expression over my cop-out. Her disappointment in me.

"What do you think, Indy? Can you fit me into your busy schedule?" Aiden jokes, glancing at Indy.

For one blink, her expression is furious. Her hurt obvious. Her shoulders tense. But then she takes a deep breath and pastes on a big smile. She glances at Aiden and her anger softens. "Of course, Aid. I'd love to go with you."

Her words pierce my chest and fill it with anger, pain, and ugly thoughts. But I deserve it. All of it. Because this is what I wanted, isn't it?

If I'm doing the right thing, why does it feel so shitty?

23

INDY

A iden's kiss goodbye glances off my cheek and I dip my head, nodding to his cheerful "see you later," as I close the door behind him. Spinning around, I sigh and wipe a hand across my forehead.

Noah's pushing me on Aiden; his being blasé and distant, is beyond confusing. In fact, it hurts. With every one of his intense glares followed by a silence I didn't understand, a tiny, sliver of hurt, like a paper cut, nicked my heart. Over the course of four hours, my entire chest throbs with disappointment, pain, and a growing swell of anger. I lift the heal of my hand to my sternum and press, hoping to dispel the anxiety spiraling throughout me as I think of my life sans Noah.

This was supposed to be casual. Yeah, right.

"What the hell is wrong with him?" Claire asks, correctly reading my thoughts.

I look up at her, noting the way her arms are crossed over her chest. Her eyes are narrowed, her lips thinning into a straight line.

"You didn't have to stay behind," I tell her.

"Fuck that. You're clearly upset."

I wince.

"Rightfully so." She jabs a finger in the air and I manage a small smile.

My favorite day of the year is over and instead of feeling warm and bursting with gratitude, I'm exhausted and freaking relieved. Even with Aiden's surprise visit and his moving news, my energy is depleted. Emotionally exhausted, physically worn, and mentally sluggish, I don't know whether I'm happy or annoyed that my cousin is joining me in my misery.

Claire wraps her arms around me in a hug and I drop my head to her shoulder, deciding I'm a tiny bit thankful for her presence. A wave of hot tears tingles behind my eyes and I squeeze them closed. What is wrong with me? I'm not usually this sensitive. This sappy. With Noah, I knew the score so why does his dismissive attitude today matter?

"Maybe he's scared?" Claire whispers.

I pull back and give her a look.

She shrugs, but the confusion in her eyes mirrors my own.

"I'm exhausted, Claire."

She nods, tipping her head to the kitchen. "Let's say good night to your parents and swipe a bottle of wine. I'll drive your car to your place. We'll drink until we pass out since your schedule is cleared for Thanksgiving break and my schedule doesn't even exist."

I manage a nod and pull myself together to whirl through the kitchen and put on a show for Mom and Dad. I'm sure they'll see straight through me. I only need to play my role well enough so that they don't ask questions. With Claire calling all sorts of attention to herself by asking my parents which wine bottle they want to give her, I kiss Mom and Dad goodbye without drawing their narrowed eyes and frowns.

Okay, so I'm definitely glad Claire is here now. Especially because ten minutes later, she drives me home, pours me wine, and doesn't give me shit for passing out before I finish the glass.

I sleep in late the following day. So late, in fact, that Claire is already gone. However, she brewed a fresh pot of coffee before she left and I love her for it. Even though I slept soundly, it was nice having someone to share a bit of my heartache with. Claire has always been more like a sister to me but I spent my teenage years as an only child, with Aiden as my closest friend. I'm unaccustomed to having a girlfriend climb into bed with me when I'm hurting or drink a bottle of wine with me because I'm angry.

It's a hell of a lot nicer than I thought it would be.

I fix a mug of coffee and plop down at the kitchen table, unable to keep my eyes open. Thank God I'm off until Monday. I can spend the weekend kicking my ass back into gear. Is my focus off because of Noah? Am I that caught up on him?

Emotion sweeps through me, making me weepy. Yes, it appears that I am.

Rolling my eyes at myself, I force myself to get up. I take a hot shower, hoping it will wake me up. But after I blow-dry my hair, I tug on clean pajamas and crawl back into bed, prepared to sleep the day away.

The incessant ringing of my phone pulls me from sleep. My eyes open slowly, each eyelid feeling like it weighs roughly the same as a sumo wrestler. I pull myself into a seated position and grope around for my phone, finding it under a pillow.

"Yeah?" I answer, my voice heavy with sleep.

"Indy?" Noah asks, a thread of concern in his tone.

"What time is it?"

"Just after six."

"At night?" I ask, alarmed that I literally slept the entire day away.

"Yeah," he says slowly. "Are you okay?"

"Yeah." I toss myself back on my pillows, wondering why he even bothered to call after he practically set me up on a date with my best friend just last night. "What do you need?" I think my abruptness startles Noah but I don't care.

Why the hell is he even calling me after being so stand-offish last night?

"Uh, nothing. I just, I wanted to check on you."

"I'm good."

"Oh. Okay, good."

Silence stretches between us, and where it used to be comfortable, it's not. It's heavy. Tense. Awkward as fuck.

Noah sighs heavily, "I'm sorry for being weird yesterday."

"It's fine," I blow him off. Sure, I'm desperate for an explanation but if it's the one I'm pretty sure he's going to give me—that he's done with me—then I'm not up for hearing it right now.

"Look, I'm close to your place. Can I swing by? Bring dinner?"

I hesitate, wondering if I even want to see him. But my stomach grumbles and I realize I haven't eaten anything today so I mutter out, "Sure."

"What are you in the mood for?"

"Pizza."

He chuckles. "Okay. I'll be there in a bit."

I hang up without saying goodbye. The tug of sleep is strong but I force myself to swing my legs over the side of my bed and stand. A wave of dizziness crashes over me and I sit back down, dropping my face into my hands. Shit, I really do need to eat something. How the heck am I so hungover from a few glasses of wine?

When the spell passes, I stand up and pull on a hoodie and some fuzzy slippers. I don't even care what I look like. I'm too tired to care. Too confused and annoyed to want to read into anything Noah says.

I just want the damn pizza.

I PULL the door open the moment he knocks.

Noah stands there, looking irritable with his dark eyes and messy hair. His winter coat is open and a plain black shirt is visible. He holds out a pizza, which I take and turn around, not bothering to say hello.

The door closes behind him and he follows me the few steps into my kitchen.

"Indy," his tone is apologetic.

I turn and glance at him.

"I'm sorry about yesterday."

"Which part?" I ask, pulling plates and cutlery out of kitchen drawers. Placing them on the table, I uncork the wine bottle Claire and I didn't finish last night and raise it.

He shakes his head so I pour a glass for myself.

Noah sits next to me and stares at me, his expression unreadable but his eyes are filled with regret. "I'm sorry I was such a dick last night."

"Okay."

"I'm serious."

I shrug and take a sip of my wine. "Whatever, Noah. Just so you know, I don't do this."

"Do what?"

"Take guys home for holidays. Thanksgiving is my holiday, it's my favorite day of the year, and it was stupid that I was excited to spend it with you. Especially when this"—I gesture between us—"isn't really a thing."

His frown deepens and his brows furrow. "I wanted to spend the day with you too. It was nice of your mom to invite me."

I take a gulp of wine this time. My skin feels hot and cold and my eyes burn. Shit, am I going to cry? What is wrong with me? I need to stop drinking.

I place my wine glass down and pop open the pizza box, sliding a slice on each of our plates.

"Indy, don't be mad. I just, I fucked up, okay?"

I look at Noah, waiting for more.

"I like being with you, Indy. A hell of a lot more than I should. And, look, we agreed from the beginning that we would keep it casual. I've got Austin bitching at me that you're not like other girls, which I know," he adds when my eyes narrow. "I've got to keep my head in the game right now. The Hawks are off to a solid start, even without my brother, and I can't let my team down. I can't afford any distractions."

"So I'm a distraction now?" I bite out, knowing that I am because he's also a big fat distraction in my life too. But am I *just* a distraction?

Noah blows out a sigh, tipping his head. "I like you, Indy. But we both know there's nothing more for us than this." He gestures between us.

"Hot sex and pizza," I surmise, taking a large bite.

He snorts but when I don't react, his face falls. He reaches out, his touch featherlight as it travels over my wrist.

I drop my head, trying to get control of my emotions. I know what Noah and I agreed to. I know I said I would let him know if I started to catch feelings and I didn't. I didn't tell him how much I looked forward to seeing him, how I began to crave the feel of his arms around me. I didn't tell him that when we had sex it started to feel more like love. Love! I cringe, chewing my pizza.

What am I supposed to do? Tell him now when he's adding distance between us that I'm falling for him? I swallow.

No way am I setting myself up for even more disappointment. I'll be fine. I'll get through this. My heart squeezes and I press my fingers into the center of my chest, trying to alleviate some of the pressure.

Noah catches the movement and I clear my throat, pulling his eyes to mine.

Forcing my expression blank, I shrug nonchalantly. "It's fine. I get it. It was fun while it lasted and we had some good times together, right?"

Noah tips his head, studying me. After a second, he nods slowly.

"Thanks for bringing this." I lift my slice of pizza in the air, folding it in half. My body starts to shut down as I force my mind to turn off my emotions. "Honestly, I'm exhausted. But, it's good we had this chat so we know where we stand. Still cool, right?"

He nods, picking up his slice. "Do you want to hang for a bit?"

I bite my bottom lip trying to keep the torrent of tears at bay. Is he kidding me? We just kind of, sort of, broke up and he wants to "hang"? My emotions pull my thoughts in contradicting directions. On the one hand, I do want him to stay. I want him to stay because he wants to be with me, not because of some stupid friends-with-benefits agreement. On the other hand, I can't wait for him to leave so I can throw myself back into my bed and sob my eyeballs out.

Clearly, that's the more rational choice. I shake my head. "I'm really not up for it."

Noah's face falls but I steel my resolve not to give in. After all, he pretty much blew me off by taking our dinner reservation and giving it to Aiden. What the hell was he even thinking?

Noah finishes his slice quickly. The chemistry between us turns stale as we both stand from my little kitchen table. How the hell did we get here? Just last week, Noah was lighting up my nights and now, he's ruining them.

I walk him to the door and pull it wide open. "See ya around, Noah."

He hesitates, shifting from one foot to the other. He works a swallow, his Adam's apple bobbing.

Please say something. Take it all back. Tell me you feel what I feel. Tell me you want this. Me.

I wait him out, my heart more hopeful than it should be.

Finally, Noah sighs and dips his head. "Good night, Indy."

I bite the corner of my mouth to keep from crying in front of him. But as soon as he clears the threshold, I close the door and lock it. My shoulders shake with the intensity of emotions I'm holding in. My stomach coils too tightly, my chest heaves with silent sobs, and a wave of nausea rolls through me.

Oh God. The first tears fall over and I drop to my knees, letting them wash through me.

I knew better than to fall for a hockey player. I knew better than to let Noah Scotch in. I went and did it anyway. And now, I'm left to pick up the pieces all over again.

24

NOAH

"Three weeks, man," my brother says through the line. He sounds good, centered.

"Yeah. Bet you're ready to be home."

"Ready to sleep in my own bed."

I chuckle but it's forced.

"What's going on, Noah?" Easton asks.

I sigh, reclining in the chair in my hotel room. Blowing out a breath, I glance out the windows, overlooking downtown Nashville. We have a game tonight and instead of focusing on that, instead of thinking about gelling with Sims and protecting our record, I'm twisted up over Indy.

Three nights ago, I let her go for good. She was furious with me. Hurt. And as much as I try, I can't stop the look on her face before she closed her apartment door from haunting me.

I swallow past the lump in my throat. I miss her.

"Noah?"

"Indy and I broke up."

"Broke up? I thought you weren't really dating."

I chew the corner of my mouth, not knowing what the hell to say. East is right. We weren't really dating.

But he's also wrong. Because I was falling in love with Indiana Merrick. I just didn't want to admit it to her.

My brother snickers.

"What?" I snap. An image of Indy flickers to mind. Her anguished expression, fighting back tears. The exhaustion that clung to her eyes. I hurt her, cut her deep, and I feel like complete shit about it.

But I feel even worse knowing that she's never going to be mine. She never was and now, there's no hope for a future with her. I fucking sabotaged that.

"What happened?" Easton asks, his tone softer.

"I was supposed to take her to The Ivy on Saturday."

"That sounds pretty serious. What went wrong?"

"I passed the reservation off to her and some guy who was making fucking heart eyes at her over Thanksgiving dinner."

Silence. For three breaths, I've stunned my brother into total silence. Then, he cracks up and I swear.

"Wait a minute, you really did that? You tried to set Indy, the girl you're fucking losing it over, up on a date?" East summarizes, howling.

"It's not funny," I retort lamely. I can't even bother to inject my tone with anger because he's right to laugh at me. I'm a laughingstock right now. A dumb one.

"You're right, you're right. It's not." Easton clears his throat before his laughter erupts again. "It's fucking hilarious! What is wrong with you, Noah?"

"I don't know," I answer honestly. What the hell is wrong with me? Indy and I made a deal, sure, but part of the deal included my taking her around modern Boston. The city side with delicious food and craft cocktails. Cool art exhibits and downtown shopping. Instead, I bailed on that too and tried to *set her up*. With a guy who makes her smile, who puts her at ease, who made her eyes light up when she saw him. A man her dad calls "son" and her mom fawns over.

A man she deserves. One who has a stable career, will be living permanently in the city, and won't spend nights at a time in other parts of the country, having random girls slip their numbers in his pockets.

"Noah," Easton's voice pulls me back to the conversation.

I grunt.

"What happened after Thanksgiving?"

"We're done." I sound as bitter as I feel. "I grabbed a pizza and stopped by her place."

"And?"

"And she pretty much said it was fun while it lasted and to have a nice life."

East whistles. "Shit. You really pissed her off, man."

"I hurt her."

Easton swears. "That's even worse."

Hanging my head, I pinch the insides of my eyes. "I know. I messaged her a few times since and…"

"She's ghosting you."

"Pretty much."

"Wow. Who knew Little Indy would hold such a grudge."

Even though Easton is trying to cheer me up, it still pisses me off that he'd say something—anything—negative about Indy. "I deserve it."

"Of course you do. You played this whole thing wrong."

I roll my eyes, shifting my weight in my chair. "Yeah? What the hell would you have done differently?"

"I would have told her how I felt. For real. The second I started having real feelings," he says easily.

"Bullshit. You would have chickened out," I call him out.

"No way, man. I've spent too much time making excuses and pushing people away. Look where it got me? If I found a woman who would really stand by me while I do all of this shit? I'd jump in with both feet."

"You're serious?"

"As a heart attack. The only difference is, I'll never find a woman who wants to put up with all my bullshit and baggage. So it's kind of a moot point."

I sigh, "East—"

"We're talking about you," my brother deflects.

I swallow, thinking over his words. "I fucked up."

"You did."

"But I did what's best for her."

"If you think so."

"We never had a future."

"If that's what you want to believe."

"What the fuck, man? Are you just going to agree with me?" I nearly shout.

East snorts. "If I disagree, will it make a difference? You've been kidding yourself since day one, Noah. This has always been a helluva lot more serious than you keep pretending."

"She doesn't want this life."

"Then let her go, Noah. Walk away. Let her go on her date to The Ivy with another guy and be happy for her."

My stomach twists in knots just thinking of Indy and Aiden going out to dinner together. Anger beads in my bloodstream, hot and jealous. What the fuck was I thinking?

"You can't, can you?" Easton goads.

"I gotta go. We got a game tonight," I bite out, desperate to end this conversation.

"If she's the one, Noah—"

"I'll see you in three weeks, East," I cut him off.

Easton sighs, "Good luck tonight, brother."

I disconnect the call and jump up from my seat, pacing back and forth in front of the hotel bed. The whole point behind a friends-with-benefits arrangement is to avoid feeling like this. Fucked up, angry, scared, jealous.

I thought that by hooking up with Indy, I'd be able to avoid distractions.

What a laughable concept.

As if I could just stop thinking about Indy. As if I could just let her go.

"GOOD GAME, SCOTCH!" Torsten slaps a palm against my helmet, whooping loudly as we skate off the ice.

We won. Thank God, we won tonight's game. The team celebrates in the locker room, all of us recounting parts of the game, telling jokes, and wishing East was here with us.

When the room starts to clear out, I pull out my phone to check it. Disappointment swirls in my stomach that there's no message from Indy. I don't know why the hell I keep hoping there will be. I really messed things up with her and even though I did what needed to be done, I don't feel relieved at all.

I feel like shit.

My stomach sinks. I plop down on the bench and tap out a message. Delete. I try again. Delete.

Damn. It's been three days since I've talked to her and it feels like the longest three days of my life.

But I didn't end things with Indy for me. I did it for her. For her future and the lifestyle she wants.

I close my eyes and drop my forehead into my hand. All I'll accomplish by messaging her is making things between us even more convoluted. What the hell am I doing besides playing juvenile head games? She needs to move on and I need to let her.

Forcing myself to stand up, I clutch my cell phone in my fist.

It beeps with an incoming message and my heart leaps into my throat. A wave of hopefulness washes through me as I bring my phone up.

The second I spot Austin's name, disappointment plows through me.

Austin: Team's grabbing beers at the hotel. Even James. You coming?

Shit. Team drinks is the last thing I feel like doing. I'm exhausted, pissed off, and in the kind of mood that will quickly put a damper on team morale.

I sigh, dropping my forehead against the locker door. The cool metal cuts into my skin as I mentally pep talk myself.

It's time for me to move on. Indy made it clear that there's nothing left between us. All we have now are a handful of good memories. That needs to be enough. I need to get my head on straight and keep moving forward.

Me: Yeah. Meet you there.

25

INDY

That can't be right.

I count back on my fingers, looking at them in utter confusion, as the math doesn't add up. At least, not the way it's supposed to.

"No. No way," I murmur, drawing Claire's stare.

"What's wrong?" she asks when she sees my expression.

"When did we get coffee with Rielle?" I ask her, vaguely recalling the afternoon in the coffee shop when I got my period. But that was weeks—no, months—ago.

"Uh..." Claire stares at me like I'm losing my mind. "Like two months ago. See what I mean? She doesn't have time for anything anymore. Can't even get a cup of coffee with her freaking friends." She stops speaking, her eyes narrowing. "Dude, what's wrong with you?"

My body locks down as my mind whirls, mentally counting and recounting. It can't be...but, shit, when the hell was my last period?

"Earth to Indy!" Claire waves a hand in front of my face.

I open my mouth but no words come out. Swiping my

tongue along my lower lip, I clear my throat. "I don't remember when I last had my period."

Claire's eyes widen and her mouth drops open. Her expression is so dramatic, so damn appropriate, that I'd laugh if we weren't talking about me.

"I mean, I do," I clarify. "It was the day we met Rielle for coffee."

"Shit, Indy." Claire drops to her knees on the floor in front of me. "That was like…" She pulls up the calendar app on her phone. "Seven weeks ago."

I close my eyes.

"It could be something else," Claire whispers.

I open my eyes and glare at her. "Like what?"

"Have you been exercising a lot lately?"

When I flip her the middle finger, she cracks a small smile and then I do and then we're both hysterically laughing, clutching our stomachs, even though nothing, not one thing, is funny at the moment. My laughter gives way to tears that turn to hiccups and then, I'm sobbing, fat tears streaming down my face as my hands shake.

"What the hell am I going to do?"

Claire hops up from her spot on the floor and grabs my house keys off my table. "Confirm it. We don't even know what we're dealing with. I'm going to run around the corner and grab some tests." She darts into my kitchen and returns with a glass of water. "You start drinking. We're going to need a lot of pee."

I wrinkle my nose. "Seriously?"

"If you want to do multiple tests."

"Right." I gulp back some water. "Go!" I usher her to the door when she pauses to stare at me.

"I'd offer wine but…" Claire shrugs sheepishly.

I throw my wallet at her head. "Get some for yourself. Get me...a Snickers bar."

Claire snorts and I crack a smile. Tears well in the corners of my eyes again and my cousin's expression softens. "No matter what happens, Indiana, we'll figure this out."

At her words, my tears spill over my eyelids. I stare at my cousin, probably less qualified to offer words of wisdom than me, but know she's being truthful. Even though Claire is a hot mess half the time, she's always had my back. She's always been there for me, like right now. And she's right, we will figure this out. Whatever *this* ends up being. "Okay."

"Okay," she says before slipping out of my apartment.

I glance at the water glass and take a deep breath. Then, I chug it.

FOUR TESTS.

Four freaking tests from four different manufacturers, which all confirm the same thing.

"You're really pregnant." Claire's voice is hushed, as if she's surprised. As if this isn't the obvious conclusion when you miss your period and are sexually active with a hunky hockey god.

"I'm really pregnant," I confirm, staring at the four positive tests.

"Are you going to tell your parents?"

I lean back against the bathroom door and slide down until I'm seated on the floor. Claire sits next to me and crosses her legs. For a moment, it's like we're kids again, playing makeup in the bathroom and making plans for when we're old enough to actually go out wearing it.

"Of course I'm going to tell them."

She nods.

"But don't you think I should tell him first?"

"Scotch?"

"No, the other guy I've been sleeping with," I deadpan and Claire snickers.

She takes my hand in hers and squeezes. "Yes, I think you should tell him first. It's the mature thing to do, the right thing, and you've always been—"

"A rule follower?"

"Well, this may change your rule-following status but…"

I laugh and Claire grins. "Tell him, Indy."

I nod, blowing out a breath. "I need to figure it out first. For myself, I mean."

"Are you going to…"

I look up at her.

"*Keep* it?" she asks softly.

It's a fair question and I appreciate the lack of judgement in Claire's tone when she asks it. But it's not a question I even consider before nodding. "I'm twenty-seven years old, Claire. I have a well-paying job, my own place, supportive parents and family." I gesture at her. "I know it's not the decision everyone would or even could make but I can and, well"—I shrug—"I always wanted to be a mom. I just thought I'd be married first."

"Or at least dating the guy," Claire supplies helpfully before wincing at her words.

"Or that," I agree. "I just, I need to sort through it in my head. How it will all work, you know? I mean, I can do this on my own for sure, but if Noah wants to be involved, he can."

Claire bites the corner of her mouth. "Talk to him, Indy."

I blow out a deep breath and pick up my phone. With shaky fingers, I tap out a message to Noah.

Me: Hey. Can we talk?

He responds immediately, which causes a flicker of relief to roll through my body.

Noah: Hi. Of course. Are you okay?

"Damn, he's intuitive," Claire remarks. "Must have gotten all the intuition in the Scotch family because his brother is oblivious to life."

Before I can formulate a response, my phone chimes again.

Noah: Do you want me to come by?

Shit. I show Claire my phone screen. "I can't. I'm not ready to talk to him about this *now*."

"Okay, that's okay."

"Plus, he has a big game tonight," I add, not wanting to deliver this news before he has to appear on ESPN. God, why does that even matter right now?

Claire takes my phone and taps out a reply, showing it to me before pressing send.

Me: I'm tied up at the moment. Can we talk later? After your game tonight?

I nod and she hits send.

Noah: You coming to the game?

Me: Yes.

Noah: Okay. Wait for me afterward? We'll grab a bite.

"Aww," Claire sighs dreamily. "He misses you, Indy."

"I'm sure he's not going to feel that way after I tell him I'm having his baby," I snap. I inhale sharply, the information finally penetrating the protective walls of my brain. "Claire, I'm having a baby."

She looks up, her eyes widening at whatever she reads on my face.

"I'm growing a *person*," I add.

Claire wraps her arm around my shoulders and I lean into

her. "You're going to be an amazing mama, Indy. Trust me." I look up at her and she grins. "I know what you're thinking but about this, you can trust me."

My phone dings again.

Noah: It's okay if you don't want to get dinner. We can just talk.

Me: We need to talk.

His response is immediate.

Noah: Indy, is everything okay?

Me: Good luck tonight. I'll meet you after the game.

I'M RELIEVED that Noah plays well. Focused and determined, he's a machine on the ice, even scoring the final goal. After not seeing him for nearly a week, I can't tear my eyes away. I watch him every second of the game with my heart in my throat and my stomach in my feet.

God, I miss him.

The few times his face appears on the jumbo screen above the ice, I wince at how exhausted he looks. Purple stamps beneath his eyes, stubble on his cheeks and chin, a severe slant to his mouth.

It doesn't diminish from his sexiness. My heart leaps at the sight of him and for the millionth time since Thanksgiving, I wish things between us were different.

The Hawks win 5–3 and the team is in a celebratory mood. The guys whoop, slapping one another's helmets and backs as they skate off the ice. Instead of joining them, Noah turns around and scans the WAGs area until his gaze collides with mine.

His expression is severe, his eyes dark. He dips his chin, letting me know we're still on to talk, and I nod. Gathering up my belongings, I wait for Claire to say goodbye to some of her friends, and then we walk to the corridor where we wait for Noah and Austin.

When the first players trickle out, my back snaps straight, anticipation and nerves riding through my veins on a wave of adrenaline.

"You got this," Claire whispers encouragingly. She tosses out hellos to the players but doesn't draw any of them into conversation like usual.

When Austin pushes through the door, I know Noah will be right behind him. Claire steps away from me and rushes for her brother, talking a mile a minute about a family drama and ushering him right past me, shooting me a wink over her shoulder.

I turn away from Claire as a shadow falls over me, two boots stopping directly in front of mine. The fresh scents of mountain air and pine wrap around me and I wish he would open his arms, scoop me up, and make me feel safe.

Because right now, I'm petrified.

"Indy." His voice is strained. He touches my wrist, hesitation and concern rippling over his expression.

"Good game, Noah." I lift the corner of my mouth but can't bring myself to smile fully and he sees it.

"What's wrong?" He inches closer, his eyes burning.

I tip my head down the hall. "Can we get out of here?"

He nods and even though we're not together, he threads his fingers with mine and leads me out of the arena, not caring who sees, not caring about anything except me.

The realization makes my eyes sting and I silently curse myself. *Pull it together, Indiana.* Today, in a crazy whirlwind where Google and SEO became my best friends, I read about the wild and unpredictable pregnancy hormones. Right now, I am that woman. Overcome with too many damn feelings to process any of them.

Noah tucks me into the passenger seat of his car and slides behind the steering wheel. He flips on the ignition and cold air immediately blasts from the vents. He flips the temperature dial all the way to hot and we sit in silence for several breaths as the car gradually warms. Noah turns to look at me, his fingertips tapping the top of the center console.

"Indy, just tell me. Are you okay?"

I nod, not trusting my voice.

"Did something happen? Are you sick?" Anguish ripples over his face, his tone pleading.

"Kind of," I manage, tears welling in my eyes.

His expression is stricken as he stares at me with wide eyes. "Baby, whatever it is, you can tell me. I don't care if we're hooking up or not, I'm here for you."

I nod, bringing my hands to my cheeks.

"Talk to me, Indy," he pleads.

I close my eyes, not wanting to see his expression as I blurt out, "I'm pregnant."

The words hover between us, causing the air to shift. Noah stops talking. I force my eyes open. His head jerks back like I pushed him and he stares at me in confusion. "Um, what?"

I work a swallow and repeat myself, relieved my voice doesn't crack. "I'm pregnant, Noah."

"A baby?"

I nod. Noah's hand slides off the center console and wraps around my wrist. Still, I can't read his thoughts other than the sheer confusion in his eyes.

"I just found out today," I add.

"Are you—"

"I'm keeping it."

He shakes his head and I flinch, ripping my wrist from him.

He grabs it again, squeezing. "That's not what I was going to ask." He dips his head to meet my eyes so I'm staring directly into his when he says, "I was going to ask if you're okay?"

I blow out a sigh, my body burning hot and cold. Nerves and fear and uncertainty swirl through my limbs with the force of a hurricane. I feel like I'm going to be sick.

"Indy?"

"I don't know." I look at him. The more seconds that tick by without him freaking out causes my emotions to swirl violently. I feel wild, out of control, scared out of my mind.

Noah's expression softens. Without hesitating, he leans over the center console and pulls me into his arms. The second my face rests against his shoulder, I breathe him in. Tears track my cheeks as I cry and Noah holds me.

"Noah, I don't know," I repeat myself.

"You are, Indy," he says without a trace of doubt. "You are."

26

NOAH

She pulls back and stares at me like she's not sure if she believes me or not.

My heart pumps furiously, my head buzzing with a million thoughts, questions, but catching the look on Indy's face, I force myself to hold them back. She's overwhelmed, fuck, I feel overwhelmed and I'm not the pregnant one.

A baby. Indy's pregnant with my baby.

I blow out a sigh. I can't think about that now. I need to keep my focus on Indy. "Are you hungry?"

She shakes her head. "Can we just, can you take me home?" Her voice is small and I hate it. I hate hearing the uncertainty there when I've come to know her as being larger than life.

"Yeah. We'll pick something up on the way to your place. You need to eat." It comes out more forceful than I intend but whatever. She does need to eat. She looks pale, exhausted...upset.

I'm going to have a baby.

The thought makes me shake my head as I pull out of the parking lot and onto the street toward Indy's place. From my peripheral vision, I notice Indy studying me but when I glance over at her, she snaps her head to the passenger window.

She's freaking out. That's normal, isn't it? To be rattled by the news that you're about to have a baby. An unplanned baby with a partner you're not even dating.

My grip tightens on the steering wheel and my molars click together. Damn it. Why the hell am I not freaking the fuck out?

Sure, I'm surprised. Shocked really. But not upset. Not rattled.

A baby. I'm going to be a father. The thought makes me grin before an image of my own dad pops into my head. I'll be nothing like him. Have I been drinking too much lately?

Oh man, I gotta call East. I bet he'll be over the moon at the news. A little dude to teach hockey to…

Wait, what if it's a girl. Well, she can play hockey too. Man, a little girl with Indy's eyes and smile.

This changes everything. Absolutely everything.

Indy and I are going to be parents. Sure, none of this is happening in the order I thought it would but it's happening. And I've always wanted kids. A whole houseful of them.

I shoot a quick glance at Indy. She's going to be an incredible mother. Everything my mom wasn't. God, our baby is already so damn lucky.

I pull into a plaza and stop in front of a sandwich and salad shop.

"What are you feeling? Do you have any cravings?" I ask.

Her mouth pulls tight as her eyes narrow at me. She shakes her head. "I'll just take…a soup."

"A soup? C'mon babe, you need more than that."

She flinches at the endearment and lets out a shaky breath. "Soup and sandwich. Not meat. Oh my God." She smacks her forehead and I frown. "I can't have lunch meat."

"What? Why?" I lean toward her.

"It could have a bacteria in it. Listeria. It could harm the baby. And no soft cheeses either, like the unpasteurized ones. I'm not supposed to sleep on my stomach anymore. How am I going to manage that when I turn in my sleep?" She raises her eyebrows at me, her eyes glossing over. "No exercising for the next two months, which I'm sure will be awesome with helping to manage my weight gain." Her nose wrinkles and she snaps her mouth shut, mashing her lips together. I reach for her hand but she pulls it away. "Just a soup, Noah."

I hate that she's stiff and unyielding around me. I can help her. We're in this together. Doesn't she understand that? Things are different now. Before, we didn't want the same things. But now, now we're having a baby. There will be plenty of time to talk everything through. Right now, I just need to take care of Indy.

Her gaze turns to outside the window again and I open the driver's side door. "Just a soup," I agree, leaving the car.

It only takes a few minutes for our order but once I'm back inside the car, the temperature has dropped. A chill exists between Indy and me that was never there before and it pisses me off. I get that she's scared, overwhelmed, but why won't she be that way *with* me? We're having a baby for crying out loud.

I pull into the parking lot next to Indy's place and she hops from the car before I even put it in park. Grabbing the takeout, I follow her into her building and up the stairs, swearing when she slips on a step.

She turns around and glares at me. I glare right back.

She's right. We definitely need to talk.

Indy pushes into her apartment and I follow behind, placing the takeout bag on the kitchen table.

Indy whirls, tapping her foot against the floor, her arms crossed over her chest. I peer at her, trying to gauge the degree of her freak-out that is clearly on the horizon. "Want to eat first?"

Her face crumples and she dips her head.

Automatically, guilt rises in my throat. "Hey, hey," I say, keeping my voice soft. But when I step toward her, her gaze snaps up and her expression has changed. Hardened. She stares at me with pinched lips and narrowed eyes.

"We need to talk, Noah," she says the words slowly but her voice doesn't crack. I can tell she's trying to keep it all together so I oblige and sit down on the couch, waiting for her to say her piece.

Indy doesn't sit; instead she paces back and forth in front of me. "I'm pregnant."

I smile. "I know."

"It's not funny."

"I'm not laughing."

She shoots me a look that would have lesser men withering. She walks to the other side of the coffee table. Spinning toward me, hands on hips, she exhales, "Okay, so, I've been thinking about this all day. I'm going to have the baby."

"Good."

"And I want you to know that I've got this."

"I trust you," I say, wondering if this is what she's after. Does she think that I don't know that she'll take good care of our baby? That she won't put the baby's needs ahead of her own?

"And I didn't plan this."

I rear back. I'd never think she deliberately tried to get pregnant. "I know that."

"Good. Okay." She nods, resuming her pacing. "Of course, you can be involved in the baby's life but I'm not saddling you with any expectations or responsibilities or—"

"What?" I snap. "What the hell are you talking about?"

She sighs, as if I've somehow inconvenienced her and I lean forward on the couch, staring at her. "Noah, I've worked my ass off for my career."

"So have I," I manage evenly, not liking where this conversation is headed.

"Well, I'm not going to drop my whole life, my career, to follow you from city to city while you play hockey."

"I'm not asking you to."

She snorts, shaking her head. "Right. Okay, good. Well, you're going to be gone for a third of the year. Plus all the training camps and fundraisers and events. So, while you're off doing your thing, the baby and I will be here doing ours and I need to figure it all out so our lives will run smoothly when you're not here to help."

Anger begins to simmer in my veins at her tone. At her implications. Does she think I'm just going to abandon her and the baby, run off and play hockey, as if they don't matter? As if they don't even exist? "What are you trying to say, Indy?"

"I'm not trying to say anything. I *am* saying that I'm making a plan for when the baby comes. I will sort out child-care and a schedule. I'll make a plan for night feedings and how to manage all the doctor appointments. I want you to know that I got this. One hundred percent. Obviously, my parents will help. And that, I'm not asking you for anything, okay? I don't need your money."

I sneer.

"Or your guilt."

"Guilt?" I stand to my feet. "Where is this coming from?"

She waves a hand at my frame. "This. I don't need the added stress of this. I just wanted to let you know."

"That's it?" I chuckle but it's hard, condescending. "You just want to tell that you're pregnant and now I can go on my merry way?"

She shrugs. "It's not like we're together, Noah."

"I know that, Indy."

"I mean, at your insistence, I have a dinner date with Aiden on Saturday." She widens her eyes at me.

I pause, glaring at her. "You're still going?"

She stares at me, incredulous and burning with frustration. "Did you think I was going to just stop having a life because I'm having a baby? What? Do you want me to throw away my career? Toss out opportunities to be in a stable relationship and create a home, a family, for my baby so I can watch you flirt with puck bunnies?"

"What are you even talking about?" I explode. Flirt with puck bunnies? Throw away her career? A fucking date with Aiden? "You're not making any sense, Indiana." I sit back down and gesture to the spot beside me, trying to stay calm, when inside, I can hear my goddamn pulse in my eardrums. She thinks I'd abandon her.

And is she fucking kidding me? Create a family with another man to raise my kid?

"I'm making plenty of sense," she throws back, walking around the coffee table again. "I'm having a baby and I'm making a plan. I'm being responsible."

My mouth drops open and I shake my head at the fury in her voice.

"Indy, this happened, okay? It's no one's fault."

Her eyes tear up as she glares at me but I can't tell if they're in anger or sadness or...pure frustration. "I know that,

Noah. I just, I need you to understand how this is going to go."

I lean back, folding my arms over my chest and flip my chin at her. "Okay. How's it going to go?"

She stops moving and faces me head-on. This time, when she speaks, her voice is clear and it scrapes at me even more. "The baby and I are going to live here. My mom will come to help me for the first few weeks as I get settled. Then, I'll look into childcare options although I'm sure once I tell my parents, Mom will offer to watch the baby while I'm at work. When you're in town, you can come over and spend time with the baby or we can arrange play dates at your house. I won't get in your way with any girls you'd like to date but I ask that you don't bring random women around our child. And I'll do the same. With men, I mean. I—"

I spring up again, cutting her off. "So you've got this all figured out, huh?" I grab my wallet and phone off the kitchen table.

"Well, yeah, Noah. I'm the one having the baby. I need to think about—"

"So, what you're saying is, you really don't need me, want me, for anything?" I spit out, praying the answer is a strong hell no. *Give me something to work with, Indy.*

Instead, Indy shrugs.

I chuckle again, striding toward the door. "Whatever, Indy. I guess you don't need anyone, right? You have all the answers, all the solutions." I reach for the doorknob, rattling it. My anger pours from my fingertips like hot water. Scalding and burning. Blistering and hurting.

"Where are you going?" Her voice wavers once and I turn around.

"It looks like you've got it all figured out. What the hell do you need me for, right? I mean, it's not like I'm the father or anything," I bite out, pulling the door wide open. "Call me when you want to have an actual conversation, Indy," I throw out over my shoulder before storming from her place.

I bound down the stairs, my head thumping. I know I'm being stupid. I should stay and talk to her, talk through this with her. But she doesn't seem interested in hearing anything I have to say.

She doesn't seem interested in anything except her goddamn schedule and life plans. None of which include me.

Throw away her career. Create a family. With another fucking man.

Is she out of her mind?

I fume, throwing myself behind the wheel of my car.

I know I messed up when I pushed Indy toward Aiden. But now that she's pregnant, things are different. I never wanted to let her go and now, no matter what, we'll always be connected.

So why the hell is she trying so hard to cut me from her life completely?

As if I don't belong in it? As if I'd even go.

27

INDY

"That's your best reaction?" Aiden goads me as he strikes another awkward, nowhere near stylish pose, in front of my apartment door.

I snort, forcing myself to smile when I really feel like crying. I haven't spoken to Noah since Thursday night and today, I regret not answering his calls and text messages.

It was stupid of my delusional heart to think the knock on the door could have been Noah. Not when Aiden messaged me that he was on his way over to pick me up for dinner.

"I'm wearing a pocket square." Aiden jabs at his chest, where I imagine he's all decked out in a fancy blazer under his winter coat. I roll my eyes and turn to grab my coat and scarf from the hook.

"What's going on with you?" Aiden asks. The door closes behind him and I wrap my scarf around my neck.

"Nothing," I sigh.

"We don't have to go tonight. I thought you'd want to get out a little. It was nice of the hockey guy to give up his reservation…"

I spin around and glare at my best friend.

"Ah, so *hockey guy* got your attention?" He smirks and it's annoying as hell.

"His name is Noah."

"And…?"

"And nothing." I shrug on my coat and button it up.

Aiden chuckles. "Yeah right, Indy. There's so much you're not telling me but it's cool…we've got all of dinner to talk about it."

I stick my tongue out at him and glide past. He chuckles as he locks my apartment door.

For the entire drive to The Ivy, my thoughts revolve around Noah. Why didn't he fight harder for me? For us? Why didn't I give him a chance to weigh in on anything? How does he even feel about me being pregnant?

Aiden grumbles next to me and I know he's trying to figure out what the hell is wrong with me. But I don't have the energy to clue him in. Right now, I'm tired. Emotionally drained and physically ill. I feel like I could cry at any second, which pisses me off and makes the tears swell stronger.

I drop my head to the cold glass of the window and watch the snow swirl outside.

"Indy?" Aiden's voice is soft. His hand finds mine and he squeezes my fingers. "Is this sass because of a guy issue or a work-related tiff? Or is it something deeper?"

I glance at him and his eyes pierce mine, filled with concern.

"You hurt, Indy girl?" he asks and I don't miss the break in his voice.

Aiden has been my go-to guy for forever. Even when we were awkward preteens and the usual puberty shit blew up between us, we managed to wade through it. But I don't know how to tell him this. I don't know how to tell anyone other than Claire because, no judgement, and Noah, because hey, he's the dad.

And look how freaking awful that turned out.

"Do you need help?" Aiden continues, the pressure of his grip increasing. His laughter from earlier has faded and now a severity I'm unfamiliar with lines his usually amiable face.

"Can we talk at The Ivy?" I ask in a small voice. I hate how unsure I sound. I hate how unconfident I feel.

"Of course, babe." Aiden gives one last squeeze before dropping my hand. "We can do whatever you want."

We drive the rest of the way in silence but once we're seated in the ridiculously trendy restaurant and I pass on wine, Aiden knows something real is up.

"What's going on?" he demands as soon as the server steps away with our drink orders.

I sigh, my best way to emote these days. My fingers fiddle with the edge of the linen napkin as I force myself to meet Aiden's gaze. "I need you to stay calm, okay?"

"Are you sick?" he blurts out, paling.

I shake my head.

"Jesus, Indy. Fine, yeah, I'll stay calm," Aiden lies.

I offer him a small smile to reassure both of us and whisper, "I'm pregnant."

Aiden stares at me in shock for two blinks before he erupts in laughter.

Laughter!

He folds to the side and shakes his head, his loud chortle drawing looks from nearby patrons. "Christ, Indiana. That was good. That was good. You really had me going. My God, you haven't put that much depth into a role since you played Scarlett O'Hara sophomore year at the—"

"I'm serious, Aid," I cut him off, irritated that he'd think I'd make this up. That I'd just invent a baby.

He pinches the insides of his eyes, his laughter trailing off.

I clear my throat.

An awkward pause hovers over the table, only broken by the impeccable timing of our server. "Do you have any questions about the menu or are you all set to order?"

"We still need a few minutes," Aiden replies, his eyes trained on me. Once she's out of earshot, Aiden hisses, "You're fucking serious?"

I nod, fisting the cloth napkin.

Aiden zeroes in on the movement and blows out a long exhale. "Who is he?"

"Who?" I ask.

"The father." He gives me an impatient look. "I swear to God, Indiana, if some asshole left you high and dry, I will—"

"It's Noah."

"The hockey guy?"

I nod and Aiden gapes.

"Wait a second." He holds up a hand. "Are you telling me that you and the hockey guy—"

"Noah."

"Had a one-night stand and you invited him to your parents' house for Thanksgiving?"

I clear my throat. "It wasn't a one-night stand."

"You're *dating* him?"

"I wouldn't say dating," I backtrack.

"Indiana, stop being coy. What the hell is going on?" Aiden demands, some color returning to his face.

"We've been seeing each other. Casually," I explain.

"How casual?"

I scrunch my nose. What kind of question is that? I err on the side of caution. "Medium."

Aiden squints at me. "You don't make any sense."

"Neither do you."

He shakes his head. "Why the hell did he give us his reservation? For a minute, it felt like he was trying to set us up. Wait a minute…" Aiden's eyes widen. "Is he trying to pawn you and the baby off?"

"Thanks a lot," I huff, now annoyed that Aiden thinks I am someone who can just be *pawned* off. With a child no less.

"Does he know about the baby?" Aiden wonders aloud.

"Did you have a chance to look over the menu?" The server returns.

I snort and Aiden glares, ordering us two steaks. "You can eat that, right?" he asks me and I nod. "I can't believe we're dining here and I didn't even look at the menu," he grumbles.

"You could have." I nudge the wine list closer to him.

He rolls his eyes and stares at me. "I want the full story, Indy. From the beginning. I want to know what's going on and then I want you to tell me exactly what you need."

His sincerity brings tears to my eyes and his expression shifts to one of horror.

"It's the hormones," I explain, dabbing my eyes with the cloth napkin. I take a deep breath and dive in. I tell Aiden all about Noah's and my arrangement. Our friendship that flourished into more. The fun we had together being tourists in Boston. Nights at Taps. Then, his awkwardness on Thanksgiving and trying to set me up with Aiden.

"I knew it!" Aiden jabs a finger in the air.

"Yeah, he wasn't very subtle," I agree.

"Why would he do that? Try to set you up? Why not just end things with you?"

I shrug but I've thought about Noah's motives a lot. Especially over the past few days. "He knows we don't want the same things. I think when he met you, and we have all this history together, he thought I'd be better off with someone like you."

Aiden catches my eyes and we stare at each other for a long beat before cracking up. "I thought this guy knew you?" Aiden wheezes. "You would be bored to death with a guy like me."

"I know, right? And you would be frustrated most of the time with a girl like me."

"Someone to organize my sock drawer? I'd be the most passive-aggressive son of a bitch on the planet."

We laugh and I roll my eyes, wiping away an errant tear.

In an instant, Aiden's expression grows serious. "Then what happened?"

"I told him," I murmur, picking at a bread roll.

Aiden watches me curiously, not saying anything for the first time in his life. It both soothes and annoys me.

"It didn't go well," I add.

"What happened?"

"He stormed off, that's what happened."

In an instant, Aiden's face flushes and his eyes narrow. "I'll track down the—"

"It wasn't like that. I think I, I think I pissed him off."

"By carrying his baby?" Aiden scoffs, clearly pissed for the both of us.

"He was fine at first. Asking about me and if I need anything..." I shake my head, furrowing my brow. "But the second I mentioned that I didn't have any expectations of him and that I'm not going to follow him all around the country, that my life is here, he got frustrated."

"Hold up." Aiden shakes his head. "What exactly did you say to Scotch?"

"I knew you knew his name." I grin. Then, I recall two

nights ago for Aiden, who grows stiffer with each word I mutter. "And then he left."

"Well of course he left, Indiana," Aiden chides me. "Are you seriously saying that if someone you were having a baby with told you exactly what it's going to be like and told you they didn't need you for anything, you wouldn't be pissed?"

"It wasn't like that—"

Aiden lifts an eyebrow.

"I was processing. Trying to make sense of everything." I stand my ground.

"And? Did you give him a chance to make sense of things?"

"He left."

Aiden gives me a look. "Has he called you at all?"

"Four times," I admit.

"And?"

"I'm not ready to talk yet."

Aiden whistles. "Damn, I forgot how you can hold a grudge."

"It's not a grudge. I'm just, I've got a lot going on at the moment, okay?"

Aiden tilts his chin toward me, his expression softening. He reaches over the table and clasps my wrist. "You do. God, Indiana. You're doing a really great job and you're going to be a really amazing mother. But you need to talk to Scotch. You need to set things straight with him and let him be involved. Even if this thing with y'all was just fun in the beginning, it's more than that now. It doesn't matter if you're together or not, you're having a baby together. You will always be in each other's lives, always be connected in some way. You don't want to start this kid's life off with two parents who can't communicate with each other."

I bite my lower lip, nodding my thanks to the server as

she drops off our entrees. After she runs through our dishes and cracks some fresh black pepper on Aiden's mashed potatoes, I say, "You're right."

"I know." He smiles at me.

"I'm scared," I admit.

"I know. But you've got this, Indy. You're going to be a kick-ass mom. And whatever you need, you know I'm always in your corner."

"I know."

"I just don't want to be there when you tell Jemmy." He points his fork at me and I snort.

"Nah, I better tell Mom and Dad with Noah, don't you think?"

"I do." Aiden cuts off a bite of steak and pops it into his mouth. He groans. "Jesus, Indy. Your man's got good taste, though. This steak is delicious."

"He's not my man."

Aiden picks up his wine glass and gestures it in my direction before taking a large gulp. "He will be."

I frown.

"Trust me, Indiana. That man was trying to set you up with *me*." He laughs again, shaking his head. "He cares about you a hell of a lot more than he let on and now that you're knocked up—"

I wince.

Aiden's smile grows larger. "Well, there's no way he's letting you go without a fight. And I happen to know that hockey guys, especially yours, can throw down when they need to."

I roll my eyes but find myself grinning back at Aiden. "You really think I'll be okay?"

"I know it." He pushes my plate toward me. "Now eat. You need to keep your energy up. Plus, no offense, but you look like shit. Guess that glow hasn't kicked in for you yet, huh?"

I flip him the finger and he laughs.

But when I take a bite of my delicious steak, I forgive Aiden. And Noah.

Because this food is amazing and right now, I don't feel like puking my guts up, so life is suddenly good again.

28

NOAH

"What are you doing?" my brother asks as wind whips around my head, traveling through the phone line.

"I'm pacing," I snap, walking back and forth in front of the tenement building.

"Huh? You okay?"

"East, I gotta tell you something."

"Okay," my brother says slowly.

"Indy's pregnant."

Silence. Silence for two paces and then fucking joy. "Holy shit! Seriously? Congratulations, man! Wow. I'm going to be the best fucking uncle that kid could ever want. Damn, man. I wish I was there with you guys. How's Indy doing? How's she feeling?"

I blow out a sigh. "She's avoiding me."

"Wait, what?" I can hear the wheels turning in Easton's head. "You pushed her away, didn't you?"

"She's on a date with Aiden."

"Shut the hell up. Noah, why is your pregnant girlfriend on a date with another man at a restaurant that you got a reservation for? What the hell is going on? Jesus, I thought my life was fucked up…"

"Thanks," I bite out, stopping to lean against a stop sign. The air is frigid cold and my toes are starting to go numb. Yet, an inferno of anger, pretty much one hundred percent of it at myself, pulses in my temples. "It's on me. I fucking pushed her to go out with Aiden and then when she found out she was pregnant, she was probably alone."

"Alone?"

"I was at the game."

"Oh."

"When we talked about it, she had everything mapped out. A whole fucking plan that barely included me. She told me she didn't want to saddle me with anything. And of course I could be involved but pretty much on her terms. Oh, and she doesn't want my money."

Easton snorts. "So, basically, she's telling you to fuck off while not really telling you to fuck off?"

"What do you mean not really? She's pushing me right out the door."

"Nah, man. If she was doing that, she might not even have told you. Or she would but not this early. Tell me, do her parents know?"

"Not yet…"

"See? You were still her first call. She's probably scared, Noah. I mean, a baby is a big fucking deal. Everything you told me about you guys indicates things are a lot more serious than either of you let on."

"True," I agree, beginning my walk again.

"Then, you push her off and try to set her up on a date with another dude."

"Biggest fucking mistake." I plop down on the front steps of her building.

"Yeah man, but you need to prove to her that she can count on you. She's not just thinking about herself now but about the baby too. If she feels like you're going to get cold feet and try to push her away, why the hell should she let you in?"

I swear, pissed off that my brother grasped the heart of the issue faster than I did. "Yeah. I think you're right."

"I am," he says with his usual self-assuredness. "Noah, get your girl. Talk to her."

"I'm still waiting for her to come home."

Easton chuckles. "Relax, man. It's only eight-thirty. She's not exactly pulling an all-nighter. You need to man up here. Tell her how you really feel and go all in. Unless, you don't want to be all in?"

"I am all fucking in!" I snap, narrowing my gaze at a car's headlights as it turns onto the street.

"See, I knew it all along. Now go get your girl."

"I think this is them. Pulling up right now," I say to Easton. "I gotta go."

"Call me later, Noah. And congratulations."

"Thanks." I hang up the phone.

The second the car pulls up in front of Indy's building, I spring to my feet. The car idles at the curb and I see Indy in the passenger seat. I watch as she unclicks her seatbelt. Her head tips back, her dark hair brushing her shoulders. She laughs at something. My hands clench into fists as I narrow my gaze, drinking in the scene like the desperate man I am.

She went on the date.

You made her go on the date!

She had fun.

Can I really deny her that? After all the stress she's carrying around, I'm going to be angry that she's laughing?

My temples throb and a hot flash blazes through my

bloodstream. Yeah, yeah I am because she should be laughing with *me*.

She leans over the center console and I stride toward the car, wanting to rip open the damn door and pull her from Aiden's kiss. But she's already opening the door, her quick hug with Aiden not developing into anything more.

She closes the door, bends down, and waves goodbye. As soon as she turns, she sees me, frozen halfway between the building and the street, and she stops.

The passenger window of the car slides down and Aiden leans forward in the driver's seat, his eyes boring into mine. He looks between me and Indy before calling out, "You good, Ind?"

She nods without turning around, her gaze still latched on me. "I'm good. 'Night, Aid."

Aiden stares at me for one long beat and something passes through his expression. It's not sinister or angry. It's… encouraging? He flips his chin at me and I nod, signaling that I've got her from here. Aiden pulls away from the curb and my eyes find Indy's.

God, she's breathtaking. Even bundled up in a winter parka and a thick scarf around her neck, her hands tucked into her coat sleeves, her feet strapped into fuzzy boots. You can barely make out her shape and still, my mouth waters.

"I miss you," I blurt out the truth.

"What are you doing here?" her voice is soft but her eyes are hard, hesitant. Fuck, I hate that I put that uncertainty there.

I tilt my head toward her building. "Can we talk inside?"

She nods and walks past me. I follow her to the door, up the winding staircase, and into her apartment. When she enters, I help her out of her coat and she turns to look at me over her shoulder.

I keep my expression as neutral as possible. I didn't come here to argue with her. I didn't come here to upset her. I came here to tell her that I'm a man. Her man. Our baby's dad. And I'm not going anywhere.

She blows out a breath, her cheeks pinking even more than they did in the cold. Once she shrugs off her coat, I hang it on the hook.

"How was your dinner?" I ask.

"Delicious." She walks into the kitchen and drops a kettle on the stove. "Tea?"

"Sure. What'd you eat?"

"Steak."

"Nice choice. And"—I work a swallow—"Aiden?"

"Steak. He ordered for us."

I frown, irritated. "Why the hell would he do a thing like that? You can order your own food, Indy."

She rolls her eyes. "Yeah, I know, thanks."

I bite down on the corner of my mouth, waiting for her to get to the point. When she doesn't say anything, just turns calmly back to the tea kettle, I snap. "Indiana, I lied to you. Again."

At that, her head whips back around. She backs up until her back rests against the countertop, her hands gripping onto the lip behind her. "Wh-what?"

"I know I said this was casual. Maybe I even believed I could do casual with you. But it was a crock of shit from the start. I've always cared about you more than I wanted to let on. We're having a baby, Indy. You're going to be a mother and I'm going to be a father and we're creating a family."

Her eyes track my every movement as I step closer to the kitchen, closer to her. I'm still dressed in my winter gear and I tug off my hat, tossing it onto her little table.

"It was stupid of me to push you and Aiden together. I

was freaking out I guess, knowing that the only life I can provide you right now is one you don't want. Going to your parents' house for Thanksgiving, seeing you light up when Aiden walked in the door, hearing about his steady, consistent job as your dad called him son bothered me. Yeah, I was fucking jealous," I admit, throwing my hands in the air.

"Of Aiden?" she asks like it's the craziest idea in the world.

I shrug, shoving a hand in my pocket and rocking back on my heels. Nothing like going all in and here we are, throwing down all our cards. "Maybe not of Aiden exactly but of the kind of guy he represents. The one who can give you the life you want, the stability, the security. But it was still stupid of me to try to push you away. After that night, I hated how distant you were toward me. It fucked with my head, messed up my play, and that was before you even told me about the baby."

We're silent for a long moment. Worries and desires coloring the kitchen with tension, anticipation, and need.

"What do you think about the baby?" she asks quietly, her eyes flaring with a hope she doesn't want to give into.

"I think that if I didn't want you, if I wasn't already in goddamn love with you, I wouldn't be so, so happy that you're having my baby." The truth tumbles out of me, raw and real.

Tears fill Indy's eyes, one spilling onto her cheek.

"No tears, Indiana," I murmur, closing the space between us. With the pad of my finger, I stop her tear, dashing it away. But then my hand is back on her skin, cupping the side of her face, my thumb swiping across her bottom lip. "No tears unless they're happy ones."

At that she breaks, dropping her head into my chest and sobbing.

"Shh, baby." I wrap my arms around her and pull her into me. "I'm not going anywhere. You're never going on another date with Aiden."

She snorts, pulling back to wipe her eyes and look up at me. "It wasn't a date. Aiden's been my best friend for years."

"I don't care. You're never going on another date with another man who isn't me again." The words come out sharper than I intend and while I expect her to give me shit for them, she grins up at me.

"What are you saying, Noah?"

"I'm saying that I fucked up and I'm sorry. But from the first time I kissed you, Indy, you've been mine. My girl." My hand drops to her still flat tummy. "Our baby. We're a family now. And I won't have any members of my family canoodling—"

"Canoodling?" She lifts an eyebrow, her eyes sparkling.

"With any other men," I finish, lifting an eyebrow.

Her expression softens and her hands come up, resting on my biceps. "I hate that you pushed me away, Noah."

"I know. It won't ever happen again."

"How do I know that?"

I sigh, knowing I need to prove my feelings to her. My brother was right; I need to man up. Can't just be all talk, no action. Sweet words, no follow through. I hold her tighter. "Give me time to show you, babe. Things between us happened fast. We just skipped a whole bunch of steps and now we're here. I can't go back and undo the past but I can prove to you going forward that I'm yours. That we will figure this out. That I don't expect you to drop your career or change your dreams because of my job. We're a team, Indy. We just need to communicate better."

She nods into my chest, the material of my jacket slipping against her chin. "So you're not going to say anything when I pack a backpack and take eight kids to South Asia in three weeks?"

I cringe. Fuck, I forgot about her trip. A flicker of worry snakes through me. How am I going to let my pregnant girl go to a developing country in her first trimester?

"Noah?" she prods.

"No, I'm going to say a lot of things, Indy." I feel her stiffen in my arms but I just hold her tighter. "But I trust you. Let's just check with a doctor first, make sure you have everything you need before your trip, and plan for the unexpected, okay?"

She wiggles in my arms until I loosen my hold. Tipping back her chin, her eyes find mine. "You're serious?"

"I'm always serious when it comes to you. How the hell do you think we ended up in this mess?"

"You're not going to try to get me to cancel the trip?"

"No. But I am going to take you to the doctor's and help you pack your bag and get you an international SIM so you can call me every day from wherever you are."

She smiles, some of the worry draining from her face. "Okay."

"Okay?"

She nods.

"And we are going to talk about all the things. Like living arrangements and childcare. Of course I want your parents to be involved. But don't for one second think that I'm not going to be actively present in my kid's life. I want to get up overnight and change diapers, make bottles, whatever. I want this with you. And I wanted it with you before you ever told me you were pregnant. I was just too fucking scared of letting you down."

Her eyes widen and her mouth drops open. "You're really serious?"

"What did I just tell you?"

She licks her bottom lip, studying me. "But, but we can't just move in together because we're having a baby."

"We're not. We're moving in together because we want to be together and our relationship is escalating to the next level. Or several levels." I stop for a moment, trying to read the emotions swirling in her eyes. "At least, I want that. To be with you. Just you."

"I want that too." Her response is automatic and with no hesitation. It makes me grin.

Dropping my head, I brush a kiss over her lips. "Good. Then, we're in agreement. We can live anywhere you want, babe."

She glances around her space.

"I'll even move in here if it makes you more comfortable."

Her face snaps back to mine. "You will?"

I shrug. "I don't care where I live as long as I'm falling asleep and waking up next to you. And I want to be with you, every night that I can, in case you need anything. Even me."

Her eyes glimmer as she bites her bottom lip. "Noah Scotch, I never took you for a romantic."

I chuckle, dropping my hands to her waist and squeezing lightly. "I have a lot to make up for, Little Indy."

She tilts her neck back. "You can start right now."

I snort but Indy isn't laughing as she lifts onto her toes and pulls me in for a kiss. A hot, passionate, desperate kiss that causes me to growl and her to sigh.

My arms encircle her waist as she arches into me. Her fingers grasp at the back of my head. Her mouth fuses with mine and I lose myself in her kiss.

"Missed you, Noah."

"Missed you more, baby." I walk her backward until we're in the doorway of her room. "Indy?"

She glances up at me, her lips red and swollen from my kiss.

"I love you."

She smiles, her expression opening, her eyes dazzling. "I love you too, Noah. I have for a while."

I drop my mouth to hers and kiss her for a long moment. She wiggles in my arms, tugging me through the doorframe.

"Wait." I break our kiss, glancing at the bed. "You sure it's"—I look down at her belly—"safe?"

She smiles and rolls her eyes. "Well, we already know what kind of parent you're going to be." She walks backward, pulling her sweater over her head as I unzip my jacket and let it fall to the floor.

"What kind is that?" I ask, losing my shirt next.

Indy drops back on her bed and gives me a coy smile. "The helicopter kind."

I laugh and shake my head but in the next moment I stop. Because staring at Indiana Merrick clad in tight jeans and a black lace bra, a surge of protectiveness swells through me. She's right. I'll do anything for her, for our baby, for my family.

I stride to the bed and dip over her frame until she lies back. Dropping next to her, I turn her face to mine and press a gentle kiss to the tip of her nose, her cheeks, her sweet mouth. "I think you might be right."

She laughs and tosses a leg over my hips, pulling me closer. "I'm always right, Noah Scotch."

I nod, falling back into her arms and letting her kiss, her touch, her sunshine draw me in. "Always," I agree.

29

INDY

It didn't all magically snap into place because Noah Scotch staked a claim where the baby and I are concerned. But it definitely got better, easier, right. In the weeks that followed our discovery, we focused on our relationship, on each other.

I started to realize that by swearing off hockey players, I was missing out. At least where Noah's concerned.

"Where do you think you're going so early?" He opens one eye, followed by the other, his voice still raspy with sleep.

"Good morning, baby." I bend down to kiss his forehead before I swipe my wallet off his nightstand.

"What time is it?" he asks, pulling himself into a seated position. The sheet slips down to his waist and I lose my breath.

"Seven. Go back to bed."

"Wait." He reaches for me and pulls himself from bed. "I'll make you coffee."

"You're sweet but I'm saving my caffeine for this afternoon when I hit a wall."

Noah frowns. "Still exhausted?"

I shrug. "To be expected according to Dr. Jensen. At least for another few weeks."

"Are you sure you want to tell your family *before* your trip to South Asia?" he asks for the third time this week.

I nod, grinning at him. No doubt, my parents are going to want me to call off my trip. I'm sure they're going to hover and be super overprotective, the same way Noah was until I dug my heels in. But this trip, my career, is on my terms. I know my body and I know how hard to push myself. Being pregnant definitely changes things but it doesn't change everything and the second everyone else wraps their head around that, the easier it will be for me. "I'm sure. We're having dinner at Mom and Dad's on ..."

"Tuesday."

"Yes." I snap my fingers. "Tomorrow."

Noah chuckles and wraps his arms around me. He pulls me against his chest and presses a kiss to my shoulder. "Sure you have to go so early?"

"Yes, I need to prep before my first lecture."

He grinds his hips against mine. "Nothing I can do to convince you to stay?"

I snort, reaching back to pinch his side. "Don't tempt me, Scotch. You know my willpower is shaky where you're concerned."

"Your willpower is tough as steel where everyone is concerned," he mutters, dropping his hold after one more kiss to the back of my neck. "Have a great morning. I'll meet you at our spot for lunch?"

"Our spot? Don't tell Torsten. But yeah, I'll be there. Hey, what's going on with Torsten anyway?" I wander into the hallway, down the stairs, and into the foyer with Noah close behind me.

"Hell if I know. Between him and my brother..." He shakes his head. "I'll hit him up, see if he wants to grab a coffee or something."

"Good." I shrug into my coat. "See you later."

"Bye, baby." Noah smiles and my chest feels melty. "Love you."

"Love you too."

For so long, too long, I avoided the kind of relationships that would lead to a deep commitment. I didn't want my chest to melt or my heart to race or my nerves to zing. But Noah drew me in from that first encounter. In fact, his first kiss pulled me under. Now, I don't even want to come up for air. Not when I can feel like this.

I smile back and leave his place, pushing into the arctic cold of December in Boston.

I walk half a block to my parked car and slip behind the steering wheel. A few months ago, a pregnancy would have rocked my world. I would have felt overwhelmed and petri-fied, knowing I was doing everything in the wrong order with no tick marks to cross off on my to-do list.

But with Noah, it's different. My hand rests against my stomach and even though I'm not showing at all, I know that my tiny baby is in there. Filling me up with confidence when I anticipated doubt, giving me an edge when I've always held back, keeping me company so I never feel alone.

I ease my car out of the parking space and head to the university. After so many years of trying to do everything the right way, in the right order, I've never felt as fulfilled as I do now. I have my dream job, my dream man, and a dream come true on the way.

NOAH IS NERVOUS.

The jittery tapping of his fingers against the island countertop along with how many times he's cleared his throat makes me smile. His vulnerability is sweet. Even I know that this—telling your girlfriend's parents that you got her pregnant—is out of the wheelhouse for a man, even one has tough as Noah. He clears his throat again, drawing a look from my dad, and takes a gulp of his beer.

"You sure you don't want a drink, Indy?" Dad asks for the second time, curiosity strong in his tone.

"I'm sure. Thanks, Dad. Are we almost ready to eat?"

"I invited Aunt Mary and Uncle Joe. They should be here with the kids any minute," Mom explains, popping a cracker topped with some fancy cranberry goat cheese on top into her mouth.

Noah chuckles under his breath. The "kids" are Austin and Claire. He relaxes slightly knowing they're coming for our announcement. My cousins already know our news, and while Austin was concerned when he first heard, he's since come around.

Mom helps herself to another cracker with cheese.

Damn, I want one. I can have one, right? I mean, it has to be pasteurized. I lean over the counter and reach for one, but when Noah's eyes nearly bug out of his head, I change course and stick with a safe square of cheddar.

Jeez. Is he going to be this paranoid and protective for the next six months?

He rounds the island and his hand comes to the small of my back and rests there, comforting.

Oh, who am I kidding? I like that he's protective of me. Just not so much when it comes to cheese…

The doorbell rings and I see the relief that floods Noah's

eyes. As Mom and Dad leave the kitchen to greet my family, I grin at Noah. "Holding up okay, Scotch?"

He yanks at the collar of his shirt. "Never been so nervous before in my life."

I cackle. He smirks and wraps his arm more firmly around me. Looking down at me, his eyes twinkle. "I love you, Little Indy. You know that, right?"

I nod. "I do."

"And I'm going to do everything I can to support you and your dreams and our baby."

"I know. I love you too, Noah. Don't worry, today is going to be fine."

He relaxes some and gives me a quick kiss on the lips. "I'm really happy we're having a baby, Indy."

"What?" Dad's voice booms behind us and Noah and I startle.

But Noah doesn't drop his hold on me. In fact, the second my Dad's voice rings out, Noah stiffens and straightens, turning to meet Dad head-on. "We were waiting until dinner but—"

"Oh my God, Indy! Is this true?" Mom beams, tears already collecting in the corners of her eyes, as she floats to me.

Tears swim in my eyes too as I laugh. "It's true, Mom. We're expecting!"

When I look back on this moment later, I think the thing that will stick with me the most is the lack of shock. I'm not saying there isn't surprise, because there is, but it's the best kind possible. It's the surprise of genuine excitement and anticipation, of family members giving all of their love and support.

Mom's arms come around me, pulling me from Noah's hold.

Aunt Mary literally jumps up and down clapping as Uncle Joe whistles loudly. Claire offers us a knowing smile and pops a bottle of champagne she pulls out of my parents' bar fridge. Austin shakes his head but he's laughing at our parents and grinning at Noah and me.

"We wanted to tell you at dinner," Noah says again, still looking at Dad. "We were waiting until Indy had the clear from her doctor before we shared our news."

"Why? Did something happen?" Mom whispers, true fear in her voice.

I shake my head but don't pull my eyes from Noah.

"I know this isn't the way you probably saw this unfolding for Indy," Noah says. Dad's eyes narrow. "But I love her, Jeremiah. I wasn't prepared for it, I didn't expect it, but I'm not ever giving up on it. On her. So, Indy and I are having a baby. And"—he flashes me a smile—"we're moving in together."

"Oh who cares where you live as long as we can see that little baby whenever we want!" Aunt Mary flicks away Noah's second announcement. "Tell us everything, Indy." Her attention turns to me. "How do you feel? Any morning sickness? Savannah gave me hell with that…"

As Mom and Aunt Mary slip into a side conversation involving their pregnancies, I focus on Dad and Noah's exchange.

"She never wanted to marry a hockey player," Dad murmurs.

"I know," Noah replies. He waits patiently for Dad to process the bomb he just dropped but he doesn't back down, doesn't drop his gaze. He just rocks back on his heels and waits.

"That Jace Edwards broke her heart."

Noah's jaw tightens. "Yeah."

Dad clasps Noah on the shoulder and looks him straight in the eye. "But you've never been a typical hockey player, Noah. I've always been proud of your success on the ice and now, I'm proud of you off of it too. Congratulations, son. Welcome to the family."

Emotion swells in my throat at the sweetest exchange in the history of my life. Top three for sure. My heart explodes for my dad, the best dad in all the land, as he welcomes Noah into our fold like it's the most natural thing to do. Except, he means it. I can tell by his body language that he means every word he says. I watch as Noah stands just a tiny bit taller, his lips twisting as he tries to control his feelings. "Thank you, sir." Noah sticks out a hand.

"Call me Jemmy, Noah." Dad swats his hand away and pulls him into a hug. "You guys are going to be fine," Dad says, patting his back. He shoots me a wink over Noah's shoulder.

I smile and blow him a kiss, knowing we're going to have a long chat about this later. Claire appears beside me and slips her hand in mine. "That went a million times better than I thought."

"I think so too," I whisper back.

"How you feeling?" Austin asks from my other side.

"Happy."

My cousins smile. Austin pulls me into a side hug. "I never thought I'd say this but you and Scotch make a really great couple."

"Thanks, Aus."

"He's good for you, Indy." Austin grins at me. "And you're really great for him."

The three of us laugh before Claire grabs a tray with the champagne flutes she poured out. "A toast!"

Of course, my family's chatter halts as everyone's eyes

swivel toward the alcohol. Claire passes out flutes, even handing one to me and winking to let me know it's non-alcoholic. Still, Noah pales and steps forward.

Claire swats his hand away. "It's fine, Noah. Non-alcoholic, sparkling wine." She points over her shoulder at the bottle on the counter.

He visibly relaxes as my family howls.

"And so it begins…" Uncle Joe tells him.

"You'll have to watch these two like a hawk," Dad agrees, pointing to Claire and me.

"Oh, don't worry about anything. Indy knows what she's doing," Aunt Mary decides, her confidence in me surprisingly unshakeable considering I slept my hangover off on her couch in club clothes only a few months ago.

Dad raises his glass toward Noah and me. "The best surprises in life are the ones you don't see coming, the ones you don't wait around for, the ones that happen with those who matter most. Family. We're so proud of you, Indiana. Always. I know you'll be an amazing mom and give your baby all the love in the world. Noah, we couldn't be happier that you're the man standing at Indy's side. Welcome, son." Tears spring to Mom and Aunt Mary's eyes and Uncle Joe clears his throat.

Claire rolls her eyes but beams at me.

"And not to make it about us," Dad continues. "But we're really ready for a grandkid!"

Austin chuckles, Uncle Joe shouts out "hear hear," and Noah wraps me in his arms.

"Cheers!" My family members clink their flutes together and everyone drinks to our health and happiness.

I snuggle deeper into Noah's embrace, sipping at my sparkling wine.

"You're the best part of my life, Indy," Noah whispers in

my ear. "Always, no matter what, forever, it's me plus you plus our baby."

I tip my head back and smile up at him. "You're such a sweet talker, Scotch."

He kisses my forehead. "How else could I have gotten you into my—"

Austin, standing the closest to us, clears his throat and Noah and I laugh.

"Oh! The roast!" Mom says moments before I notice the smoke coming out of the oven door. Mom lunges for it and the kitchen begins to fill with smoke.

Aunt Mary runs for the windows. The smoke detector begins to beep, filling the kitchen with a loud sound.

Claire throws her head back and laughs, filling her champagne flute.

"I'll order some pizzas," Dad says, pulling his phone from his pocket. He glances at me. "Can you eat pizza, Indy?"

"Yes, Daddy."

He smiles. "Love you, kid."

"Love you more."

Noah's hands settle on my hips as I tilt my head back once more. "Welcome to the chaos, Noah."

"Oh, it's gonna get a lot more chaotic than this," Uncle Joe says, looking pointedly at my stomach.

"I can't wait," Noah says, kissing the top of my head.

I know he means it. All of it.

I can't wait either.

30

NOAH

ONE WEEK LATER

"You sure you got everything?" I ask for the third time since we arrived at the airport.

Indy grins at me. "I'm sure. Honestly, you don't have to worry."

"I'll always worry," I mutter, checking out the students she's traveling with. Two of the guys seem strong enough to lift her in an emergency and one of the girls definitely ticks all the boxes in the over-preparedness column. Still, anxiety threads through my limbs, making me jittery with worry.

Indy's palm cups my cheek and I drag my eyes back to her. "I love that you worry."

"You hate it. You're just saying that to make me feel better."

She wrinkles her nose. "I love you."

I press a quick kiss to her lips. "I love you more."

"I'll never get tired of hearing it."

"I'll never get tired of saying it."

"Jesus, stop before I puke," Claire's voice rings out.

We turn and notice Claire standing beside us, her arms crossed against her chest.

"Sorry." Indy blushes.

"He's not." Claire hooks a thumb in my direction.

I chuckle. "You're right."

"You good, Indy?" Claire asks her cousin.

Indy nods, doing a once-over of her group. "Yeah. We're all set." She kisses Claire's cheek, wraps her arms around me for one last kiss goodbye, and steps back. "See you in ten days."

"Ten days," I confirm.

Then I watch as the woman I am so goddamn twisted up over turns around, claps her hands, and calls out to her students. They follow her in awe, their faces lighting up in excitement. They toss last waves over their shoulders to their parents as they all pass through security.

Claire and I watch until the group is out of sight.

Then, Claire clasps my shoulder. "You're going to be okay, Scotch. Trust Indy, she's the most trustworthy person on the planet."

I chuckle. "Yeah, I know. It's just, damn, I never thought I'd feel this way."

Claire peers at me, frowning. "Simultaneously giddy and tortured? Like your head is a mess but also the clearest it's ever been?"

My eyebrows furrow as I meet her gaze. I never expected Claire to hit the nail on the head before. "Well...yeah."

She sighs, "It doesn't get any easier, my friend. You just get better at managing it. And with Indy, well, you know how she feels about you. And she needs to be able to count on you to manage"—she pauses, gesturing to my being—"all of this."

"She can," I say more defensively than I'd like.

Claire snorts. "Trust me, I know, she knows, everyone knows."

"Good."

Claire nods. "Come on, let's get out of here. I'm starving."

"Are you trying to fish for an invitation to lunch?"

Claire threads her arm through mine. "Sometimes, you just get me, Scotch."

I chuckle, heading back toward the parking garage with Claire. "Hey, Easton's coming home next week."

Claire stiffens, her pace slowing as she peers up at me. "For good?"

I don't miss the hesitation in her eyes or the waver in her voice. "Yeah. For good." I tug her along. "And you need to manage all of this." I wave my empty hand at her. "Don't go tormenting my brother with your flirtatious giggles and big eyes. He needs to stay focused on his recovery."

She gasps and for a moment, I think I truly offended her. "I never tried to distract him like that."

I give her a look, snickering. "Relax, Claire, I'm playing with you. I know that. I just meant, East's going to be out of sorts for a bit. Maybe not even acting like himself. So just, you know, go easy on him."

She nods, her expression more serious than I've ever seen it. Then, she grins and a flash of humor flares in her eyes. "You mean like how I'm always giving shit to Big Daddy?" she asks, referencing her nickname for Torsten since he's the oldest guy on the team.

"Exactly like that." We step into the parking garage and walk to my car.

I slip into the driver's seat just as my phone chimes with a text. Pulling it out of my pocket, I can't stop the grin on my face when I see Indy's name.

Indy: Thanks for dropping me at the airport.

Me: As if I wouldn't see you off.

Indy: I'll miss you a whole lot, Noah. Already do.

Me: I can make up a story and halt the plane.

Indy: [3 laughing emojis] Don't you dare. I'll be back in ten days.

Me: Already counting down.

Claire huffs beside me but I hear the amusement in her tone and don't bother looking over. I keep my eyes glued to the bubbles bouncing on the bottom of my screen until Indy's message comes through.

Indy: Will you be at my place—permanently—by the time I land?

I pause. I'm desperate to move in with Indy but I also don't want to leave my brother hanging the week he comes home from rehab. Still, I know Easton will understand, will want me to be at Indy's place, especially now that she's expecting.

Me: I'm aiming for it, babe. Just need to get East settled.

Indy: Of course. I didn't mean to put you in a position where you feel torn.

Me: I know you didn't. This is why I love you.

Indy: Why?

Me: Fishing for reassurances?

Indy: No, I just like hearing you say them.

Me: There are too many ways but the biggest one of all is because you're you. Always and no matter what, you are the most confident, sincere, caring, genuine person I know. And I like who I am a hell of a lot more now that I'm with you.

Indy: Oh my God! I'm crying.

Crying? Panic seizes up in my chest.

Me: What? Why? You okay?

Indy: [laughing emoji] I'm fine. It's the hormones. And you being sweet. Gah, you make me gushy.

Me: Save it for ten days, baby. Can't wait 'til you're back. Have the best trip and safe travels.

Indy: I love you, Noah Scotch.

Me: I love you, Indiana Merrick.

Indy: Boarding now. Message when I land. XO

Me: Stay safe, my love.

I stow my phone in the cup holder and meet Claire's amused smirk.

"I need a man who looks that giddy just by texting me," she declares.

I snort, flipping the ignition on the car. "Gotta find a hockey player, Claire."

Claire flips me the bird and I laugh as I pull out of the airport parking garage. As I point the car toward the restaurant, I tell Claire to call Austin and see if he wants to meet us. While I'm so proud of Indy for pursuing her career and following her dreams, I already miss my girl. I miss being able to kiss her neck and place my palm on the softest swell of her belly.

I miss her more than I ever thought possible.

And that makes me the luckiest guy in the world.

EPILOGUE
EASTON

"Take care of yourself, man." Clint at the front desk raises a hand in farewell as I shoulder my bag.

"Yeah. Thanks for everything, dude," I call out as I pass by his desk toward the front doors of the rehab center.

The sunlight filters in through the doors and the sky gleams blue but I know it's going to be bitterly cold when I step through them. I can't fucking wait. After ninety days in rehab, I'm finally going home.

Right before I reach the doors, the small waiting room to my right explodes with applause and I turn, doing a double take when I see my brother Noah, his girl Indy, and my best friend Austin and his family sitting there.

"What are you guys doing here?" I ask, rounding the curve to where they clap.

Noah gives me a look. "Come on, man, did you think you were just going to walk out of here?"

"That we wouldn't want to congratulate you?" Mary, Austin's mom asks, a thread of hurt in her voice.

I open my arms and Mary comes forward for a hug. She's

been a second mother to me—scratch that—a real mother to me, since I was a teenager and disappointing her usually hurts more than disappointing myself. "How are you?" she whispers.

"Pretty good, Mary."

She pats my back and I release her. "I can't believe you're all here." I dip my head and scratch along my jaw to hide how much their presence affects me. Why the hell do they always think the best of me? Even when I keep proving them wrong?

"Well, we are," Joe, Austin's dad says, shaking my hand before grabbing my bag.

"I got that."

He waves me away and tucks Mary under his arm. "We'll be waiting near the cars." He turns to me. "Welcome back, East. I'm glad to see you looking so well."

I nod, my chest tightening at his words. Joe and Mary's acceptance of me, their encouragement, and constant support makes the ache there deeper. I know I've let them down. I don't want to do it again.

I turn back to my brother, Indy, Austin, and...Claire. I freeze, my breath lodging in my throat. She steps out slowly from behind her brother's frame and I wonder how the hell I didn't notice her first.

It's impossible not to notice her. She's gorgeous. Perfect. Every man's fantasy come to life but so much more than that. She's funny and witty. Playful and engaging. And...here.

I narrow my eyes. Why the hell is she here? How many people do I have to disappoint today by being the asshole who got tossed in rehab for a second time, practically ruining my NHL career?

Claire drops her eyes to the ground and I look away.

"You look good, East." My brother clasps his hand on my shoulder before pulling me into a man hug. "Happy you're home."

"Thanks, Noah." I smack my brother's back before turning to his girl who I haven't seen in ages. I mean, I saw her a handful of months ago but I haven't really spoken to her in years. "Hey Indy."

She smiles softly, wrapping her arms around my waist. "Good to see you, Easton."

I wrap my arm around her and don't miss the way my brother's eyes widen, filled with happiness at seeing me get along with his girl. His pregnant girl who I know he wants to make his wifey. Damn, seeing Noah be so open with his emotions hits me with a pang. He's healing, moving on from our parents' bullshit, while I'm here, still struggling like always.

Indy slips away and begins to shrug into her coat, my brother quick to help her.

Austin shakes my hand and bangs his fist against my shoulder, grinning at me. "Team's missed you."

I nod and chuckle, the feeling in my chest giving way to a blaze of panic.

The team? Do they even want me back after how everything went down? Aren't they going to keep the new guy Sims playing in my position? At least Sims is reliable, dependable; he fucking shows up.

"No pressure but we'd love to have you back at practice whenever you're ready."

I nod, clearing my throat. "Hell yeah, man. Can't wait to get back on the ice." It's the truth; I really can't wait to get back on the ice. But it's not the full truth. Because then I'd have to admit that I'm petrified to get back on the ice in front of thousands of people and listen to all their jeers and taunts and fuck, my stomach feels slick, I don't know if I'm ready for that.

I turn my attention to Claire. She offers me a small wave and an unsteady smile. It pisses me off the second I see it because there's nothing unsure about Claire. The girl straight up oozes confidence, calls people out on their bullshit, and never seems off balance, or hesitant, the way she is right now. "What are you doing here?" I ask.

She stiffens at my tone and I hear the inhale she sucks in. Her eyes narrow and a thrill shoots through me. There she is. "Came to see you."

"Why?" I shoulder my bag again.

She crosses her arms, staring at me. "Because I'm not a dick." She pushes past me and I snicker, keeping my back to her.

If only Claire knew how much she gets under my skin. If she had any idea how much I feel for her, how much I crave her, she wouldn't understand why I've spent years of my life keeping her at arm's length.

It's for the best.

Claire is my best friend's little sister.

She's larger than life, outgoing, and authentic.

The last thing she needs is an alcoholic who keeps falling off the wagon.

After all, it's only a matter of time 'til I'm back here. With so many people on my list to let down and disappoint, I'm not in the mood to add another.

Definitely not Claire Merrick.

WANT MORE EASTON AND CLAIRE? Find out what happens when Claire becomes Easton's new roommate and blurs all the lines in *The Risk Taker*, releasing March 1! Preorder Now!

HEY READER!

Hi there!

Thank you so much for reading *The Sweet Talker!* I hope you loved Noah and Indy's story. I'd love to know your thoughts so please consider leaving a *review*. If you adored Noah, you won't want to miss Easton's story. *The Risk Taker* is now available for preorder.

If you're interested in learning more about my books, please sign up for my monthly newsletter. It's full of updates, sales, free reads, and a new romantic, military suspense serial, *Protecting Amie*. Or, come hang out in my Facebook Reader Group, Gina's Group for Book Gossip.

Keep turning the pages to check out my other books and read a snippet of *Broken Lies*, an angsty Hollywood Romance.

Thank you so much for all of your support.

XO,
　　Gina

BROKEN LIES
ZOE

Two truths and a lie.

Moments ago, Eli Holt, famous Hollywood heartthrob, walked into Shooters Pub and discarded his winter coat and scarf in a booth.

My best friend and co-worker, Charlie, may pass out from excitement.

Meh. Holt doesn't really do it for me.

Liar.

Eli Holt does it for every legally aged vagina in the universe, and a significant number of penises too.

Holt is larger than life, his presence sucking the oxygen straight from the pub. Not just because he's the sexiest man to ever grace this bar — which he is — but because he's a bona fide celebrity hailing from the same streets of our nondescript Chicago suburb.

Even though I don't follow the celebrity news printed in *Gossip* or care about who's dating who in a circle I don't understand, I'd have to be living under a rock to overlook Holt's rugged good looks and dedication to his craft.

He turns toward me, setting off in the direction of the bar, and tugs some of his merino wool sweater up on his forearms. I nearly drool; hard muscle, corded veins, strong hands… where the hell did my chill disappear to?

Green eyes latch onto mine, amiable yet aloof, both present and not. Still, my heart stutters in my chest as his eyes slowly peruse my face, like he's trying to gauge my reaction to him, maybe wondering if I recognize him. Thick, brown hair, cut close to his scalp on the sides and left longer on top, is perfectly styled. Several days of stubble coat his steel jawline, adding an edginess that speaks to the playboy persona celebrated in the tabloids.

He saunters closer, his bulging biceps and strong back pulling at the merino wool, stretching it. Appreciation causes the corners of my mouth to tick up as I drink in his traps and lats the way an art collector salivates over a Basquiat. This man is a rare commodity, a contemporary Adonis, a perfect specimen of male anatomy.

"Hey, can I get a beer?" Fred, one of the regulars, shakes his empty pint glass.

"Not now, Fred," Charlie answers, never dragging her eyes away from the sex god who approaches the bar, commanding the space around him like a drill sergeant.

Heads swivel in his direction. While a logical part of my brain acknowledges it's because he's famous, the nerves and energy dancing around my stomach also know it's because he looks like every bad decision every woman's been tempted to make. At least once.

Green eyes pierce me to my core, causing Charlie to jab me in the ribs with her index finger. "He's going to talk to you," she whisper-hisses.

He stops in front of me, dropping his elbows to the bar. "Hey. A bucket of Heinekens and three shots of your top tequila." His voice is low and rumbly, tugging on the strings that hold my pelvic floor in place.

Jeez Louise.

A full mouth parts, revealing straight, blindingly white teeth. A nose that's been broken at least once somehow adds more character to his face instead of detracting from his rugged good looks. Full eyebrows, a teeny cleft in his chin, a barely noticeable scar above the right corner of his mouth.

"Hey babe. Did you hear me?" He snaps his fingers and my mouth drops open.

Shocked, amused, and a tiny bit embarrassed, I laugh out, "Did you just snap at me?"

"Just getting your attention."

I roll my eyes. "You have the attention of everyone in here."

He shrugs, a playful gleam ringing his irises. "We can take a selfie if you want, so you can study it later in your bedroom."

This time, laughter shoots from my mouth in surprise. Is this guy for real? "Ah, now you had to go and ruin it."

He frowns, a small dip appearing between his eyebrows. "Ruin what?"

"The fantasy playing out in my head." I joke easily, falling back into my role as bartender: engaging, playful, flippant. Grabbing three shot glasses with my right hand and swinging to pull down a bottle of top-shelf tequila with my left, I line up the glasses as I glance at Holt, "You killed it."

One side of his mouth lifts in amusement, his eyes crinkling. "That was never my intention. Now, I'll have to figure out how to get back in your good graces."

I shake my head. "What's the saying about a first impression? You only get one?"

His smile widens.

"That was your one shot to try to pick me up," I continue, unabashedly enjoying our banter as I grab a shaker. "Chilled?"

He nods, leaning closer. Rolling his lips together as if to contain his laughter, his eyes widen with curiosity that washes over me like approval. Like I really earned his attention. "Sweetheart, you would know if I was picking you up. And there wouldn't be any trying on my part." He pulls out his wallet from the back pocket of his designer distressed jeans and places it on top of the bar.

"Ouch," I grin, pouring his shots, enjoying this banter way more than I should. I mean, what kind of a woman brazenly jokes with a Hollywood actor? *The* Hollywood actor? Even though his words just shot me down, they were playful, and his attention never wavered from my face. In fact, with each passing second, his aloofness gives way to friendliness. "Well, I'm sure the women here can't wait to welcome you home with open arms."

He pulls a black AmEx from his wallet and pauses, his mouth curling into a smirk. "I'm just meeting my brother and friend for drinks. If I was looking for a real homecoming, I wouldn't be here. I'd be downtown at Lush." He tilts his head, his gaze still on mine, as he mentions the lavish nightclub known for its exclusivity and bottle service.

I smirk back, winking at him. "The night's still young, Hollywood. I'll have someone bring over your shots and beers." I grasp his credit card and turn, about to start a tab for his table.

I feel his gaze, electric and searching, settle between my shoulder blades, but I refuse to give him the chance to ruin the flirty exchange we just had. I'd never admit it out loud, but it's the type of memory I'll play over in my mind.

"Holy shit." Charlie bumps her hip against mine once Holt is gone. "Eli Holt looked like he wanted to reach over the bar and tear your clothes off."

"That's unbelievably dramatic, even for you." I move over to the ice chest to shovel ice into a bucket.

"No, I'm serious. He was into you."

I shake my head and roll my eyes. "He's a Hollywood A-lister, Charlie. Engaging with people is probably one of his job requirements."

"He didn't look over at me like that. And I'm a real fan." She huffs, pointing at herself before brandishing her index finger in my face. "You should go talk to him. Maybe even go home with him. That was one hell of a meet cute."

Cracking up at her forward, not to mention ridiculous, suggestion, I grip bottles of Heineken by their necks and bury them in the ice bucket. "You're officially banned from watching any more romantic comedies on Netflix. Besides, he said if he wanted to go home with a woman tonight, he'd be at Lush."

"Damn." Charlie frowns and then shakes her head, glancing at him seated in his booth. "I don't think he meant it."

"*Charlie.*"

"Look, all I'm saying is that you need to have fun. The past few months have been super scary for you –"

"I'm fine." I cut her off so we don't have to have this conversation again.

"I know you're fine. It was just a cyst. But it really spooked you." Charlie lowers her voice, her touch on my forearm filled with sympathy that I shake off.

"Of course it spooked me, Charlie. With my family history and Dad's vision worsening —" I pause, my hand slipping into the back pocket of my jeans. My fingertips collide with the sharp point of the folded-up paper containing my BRCA gene test results to see if I have the mutation that causes an increased risk of breast and ovarian cancers.

I've been carrying it around for nine days and still haven't worked up the courage to share my results with Dad. Or Charlie.

"I know. I didn't mean it like that. I just meant, what's the harm in having some fun? You're always talking about your business and work as the reasons why you can't seriously date. You always say you just want the casual, no-strings-attached guy."

I raise my eyebrows at her, beseeching her to make her point.

She tips her chin at the booth where Holt sits, scrolling on his phone. "What could be more fun and have fewer strings than him?"

I laugh at the absurdity of her explanation. "I love you for looking out for me. But Eli Holt is, well…" I wave a hand in his general direction, "him. And I'm me. I enjoyed our little banter at the bar, but that's the end of it. Here, deliver these to his table." I solidify my point by pressing the tray of shot glasses in her hands.

She sighs, turning toward Eli's booth, the tray balanced on her palm.

However, as she approaches his table and laughs at whatever he says, a pang of curiosity cuts through my chest.

What's so funny? What are they talking about?

Oh my God, Zo! He's here for a drink. You're a bartender.

Your exchange meant nothing. To him or to you.

Forcing myself to get back to work, I slide a free bourbon

toward Fred for his patience and scan the bar for other customers.

Read Broken Lies now!

ALSO BY GINA AZZI

Boston Hawks Hockey:

The Sweet Talker (Jan 27)

The Risk Taker (March 1)

The Faker (April 21)

Second Chance Chicago Series:

Broken Lies

Twisted Truths

Saving My Soul

Healing My Heart

The Kane Brothers Series:

Rescuing Broken (Jax's Story)

Recovering Beauty (Carter's Story)

Reclaiming Brave (Denver's Story)

My Christmas Wish

(A Kane Family Christmas

+ *One Last Chance* FREE prequel)

Finding Love in Scotland Series:

My Christmas Wish

(A Kane Family Christmas

+ *One Last Chance* FREE prequel)

One Last Chance (Daisy and Finn)

This Time Around (Aaron and Everly)

The College Pact Series:

The Last First Game (Lila's Story)

Kiss Me Goodnight in Rome (Mia's Story)

All the While (Maura's Story)

Me + You (Emma's Story)

Standalone

Corner of Ocean and Bay

ACKNOWLEDGMENTS

I dove into this series hard and enjoyed every minute of writing *The Sweet Talker*. As always, there are some very special people to thank. Without them, this book would never have come to fruition.

To Becca Mysoor - THANK YOU! Chatting and plotting with you is one of the most enjoyable parts of writing a new book. I love your energy, your constant support, but most of all, your friendship.

Erica Russikoff - I'm so grateful we connected (thanks Becca!) this year. Your feedback on Noah and Indy's story were so valuable to me. Thank you.

Virginia Carey - You're amazing! Thank you for your attention to detail, sharp eye, and quick reading. The turn-around for this book was fast and you were so on it!

Kate Farlow, Y'all. That Graphic. - What can I say? I adore these covers but even more, am so grateful for your help navigating the cover process. I know I didn't make it easy with all the changes but in the end, I'm so proud of this book and it wouldn't be what it is without your creative design. Thanks!

To Give Me Books Promotions and Candi Kane PR - A million thank yous for all of your support, organizational skills, and help in launching this book baby into the world. I love working with you ladies.

To the best ever, MPP, THANK YOU for everything. I would drop all the balls without your keeping them up in the air. I adore you much.

To RAM 2020, especially Skye and Becca - all my heartfelt thanks. The conference is incredible, the knowledge is invaluable, the friendships are priceless, and the motivation is so necessary and appreciated as we roll into 2021.

To my family, Tony, Aiva, Rome, and Luna - all my love always. You make my world go round.

ABOUT THE AUTHOR

Gina Azzi writes Contemporary Romance with relatable, genuine characters experiencing real life, love, friendships, and obstacles. She is the author of *Boston Hawks Hockey series, Second Chance Chicago series, Finding Love in Scotland series, The Kane Brothers series, The College Pact series, and Corner of Ocean and Bay.*

A Jersey girl at heart, Gina has spent her twenties traveling the world, living and working abroad, before settling down in Ontario, Canada with her husband and three children. She's a voracious reader, daydreamer, and coffee enthusiast who loves meeting new people. Say hey to her on social media or through www.ginaazzi.com.

For more information, connect with Gina here:
Join her newsletter to receive book updates, bonus content, and more!
Email: ginaazziauthor@gmail.com
Twitter: @gina_azzi
Instagram: @gina_azzi
Facebook: https://www.facebook.com/ginaazziauthor
Website: www.ginaazzi.com

Made in the USA
Monee, IL
12 February 2021